A Spirited Delusion

A Midlife is Murder Paranormal
Cozy Mystery
Clare Lockhart

Apatite Publishing

Clarity Book Cover Designs

A SPIRITED DELUSION/Clare Lockhart

For Adele Zahara, a friend through many decades.

Also by Clare Lockhart

Midlife is Murder
Paranormal Cozy Mystery Series

Midlife is Magic
Paranormal Cozy Mystery Series

Chapter One

MY EYES FLUTTERED SHUT as I let go of the last bit of tension in my body and listened to the velvety voice of Georgina, my hypnotist.

"Picture a beautiful staircase," she said. "The banister is smooth and polished. You put your hand on it and feel safe and secure. As you go down the stairs, you become more relaxed and comfortable."

Following her instructions, I visualized a staircase. Step-by-step, my limbs grew heavy as I descended.

"In front of you is a door," she said in a purring tone. "On the other side are the answers you're looking for."

Gosh, I hope so. The recliner made it easy to relax. Georgina had even provided a blanket, so I felt warm and cozy. I pictured a door, sunshine yellow, on a beach.

"Take a deep breath and go through the doorway." Georgina paused.

The warm sand pressed between my toes as I moved forward into my imaginary world.

"You've now entered a place where dreams and reality blend together. You are even more relaxed here."

Dreams and reality blend together. That notion made me uneasy. I tried not to think too much about what it might mean, considering my past. I'd learned, but not firsthand thankfully, that dreams could be doorways into other worlds, an experience I did *not* covet. Today, I was looking for a specific answer, so I pushed everything else from my mind and listened to my therapist.

Inside my head, a scene formed, a misty beach where I could hardly make out the horizon over the water. To my left, the rising sun cast a pink hazy glow.

"Think back to the dream you want to remember," she said. "Now, picture yourself inside that dream. Feel yourself there."

I exhaled slowly and recalled Georgina's promise that this dream-recall hypnosis was utterly safe because the dream I'd had three nights ago had been more like a nightmare. Of course, it was safe, I told myself, but doubt still niggled me. Just because Brielle, my twin from a parallel world, crossed into my life when she dreamed, didn't mean I was traveling the galaxies when I hit the pillow at night. And just because Brielle could physically interact with things in my life didn't mean I could do the same. It didn't mean I'd done damage in some other universe.

I just had to be sure.

Since I was trying to confirm that I *didn't* dream-travel to parallel worlds, I made myself step inside the memory of the dream I'd had three nights ago. It might be the only way to get it out of my head. I'd never had a dream like that—so real and shocking. I hadn't been able to concentrate on anything else since.

It's okay. Step into the dream.

"Think about where you are, what you see, feel, and smell," Georgina said. "If you like, you can tell me about it or just experience it quietly."

I hadn't told her any specifics, just that the dream had unsettled me. I didn't want to share details and open the door for a conversation about my paranormal life. "It's too misty for me to see much of anything."

"That's okay. Try walking through the mist. Take your time. Some images might become clearer after our session."

I pictured myself moving forward, walking along the beach, breathing in the moist air and feeling a cool vapor settle on my arms. The sky lightened, but the clouds remained, and the wind picked up as if a storm was coming. A gust blew over my face, carrying the scent of algae and ruffling my hair. Maybe because it had been unseasonably cold that spring, I thought about November gales when the fiery Lake Superior drew award-winning photographers to catch the unpredictable storms some people called witches.

Don't think about witches.

"You recall your dream in great detail," Georgina prompted, which seemed true.

A gull's scream cut across the water. At least I thought it was a gull. *Was it?*

"I think I see something," I said, moving toward a dark shape on the shore. Was I getting closer to the horrible murder I'd seen in my dream?

My shoulders tensed. I took a deep breath and willed myself to relax on the exhale. Since this was a dream vision, it was possible that whatever was up ahead still wouldn't make sense.

Or maybe everything would be obvious.

I braced myself and recalled what I'd learned—that dreams about murder were symbolic and might represent my aggression or anger toward someone. If that was true, and since I hadn't seen the face of the murdered person, I didn't know who the recipient of my anger was. I couldn't think of anyone I was that furious at and certainly no one I wished dead. Not even my cheating ex-husband, who I hardly thought about anymore. So why would I dream such a horrible thing?

I wasn't even positive I'd been the killer in the dream. Maybe I'd just been seeing things up close. That was the question haunting me, so I wanted a better look at the hands of the murderer to know for sure.

"Move toward whatever it is so you can have a look." Georgina's voice seemed far away. "Remember, nothing can hurt you. You're just a spectator."

A good thing to keep in mind. I moved closer to the large, dark object lying half on the beach and half in the water. The mist lifted, revealing a rowboat. A narrow one, perhaps used for racing. The bow was caught in the branches of a fallen tree as if the boat had drifted to shore. It looked expensive. Gleaming wood floor, seats, and gunwales. But where were the oars? Who would abandon a boat like this?

"I've come across a boat, but that's all I see." I scanned the beach, looking for the owner, but no one was nearby. At the end of the cove, off in the distance, a piece of the land jutted out like a long, green finger. For a moment, I wasn't sure I wanted to find the person who owned this boat. But avoiding the issue wouldn't do any good. The whole point was to learn who'd been on this beach. And this hypnotism seemed to work, so I'd better look around.

"This place is familiar," I said, recognizing the shape of the sheltered cove. "I think I've been here before, but not recently." The cove wasn't the one near my café in Bookend Bay, and it wasn't at Beach Meadows, in the park where I'd lived last summer. I knew those beaches like the back of my hand. I cringed at the thought of that cliché, praying I'd not see the backs of my hands forcing anyone under the water in this dream world.

"Don't overthink," Georgina said. "Allow yourself to sink deeper. You may even feel a sense of excitement."

I don't know if I'd call what I was feeling excitement. More like trepidation. "Okay," I said, unfurling my fingers. I looked inside the boat and realized everything was wet. No wonder the wood was gleaming.

As I leaned over to peer at the water sitting in the bottom, a shadow shape formed, reflecting off the surface as the sky lightened. Startled, I flinched. The figure flinched, too. I swallowed. *Holy cow.*

It was me, I realized, with relief. Just to be safe, I looked behind me. Nothing.

"You look startled, Quinn. What are you seeing?"

I let out my breath. "Nothing, just my own reflection."

Georgina said something else, but I didn't pay attention. I was starting to find her voice a distraction. She was pulling me out of this place. I stepped over the tree and walked farther down the shoreline, stepping around grasses and over driftwood. A flash of orange caught my eye. There, in the bushes, something caught on a branch.

I moved closer to see what it was.

A glove, with a thick stripe of orange across the back. It looked large, bigger than what I would wear. I'd seen these gloves before. My heart started to pound.

The gull cried again, although maybe it wasn't the gull at all. Maybe the cry came from my own throat.

The nightmare came back to me. This glove had pressed the back of someone's head under the water. Held them there.

My own hands were gripping the arm of the recliner. I cried out.

"Quinn, it's time for you to return to this room," Georgina said from a distance. "Feel yourself coming back into your body."

I focused on her voice.

"I'm going to count to five and with every number, you will feel more and more relaxed. When I reach five, you'll feel at peace and happy. You'll remember what you saw, but it won't upset you. One..."

As I concentrated on each number, it was as if I was swimming out of the dream world and surfacing into the chair in Georgina's office.

"Begin to stretch slowly, then open your eyes. You're feeling happy and refreshed," she said cheerfully.

The pull of my back muscles as I stretched was grounding. I opened my eyes, feeling calm and present in the room.

"Good. You're back." Georgina leaned forward in her chair, her ruby lips lifted in a reassuring smile. "You looked stressed, so I thought it best to end the session. I hope you don't mind my bringing you back. How are you feeling?"

"I feel fine, thank you, and it's not a problem that you ended the session. I'm going to let things resonate, but I think this was a productive experience. Thank you, again, Georgina."

I moved the chair out of its reclined position and stood. Surprisingly, the shock and fear I'd felt a minute ago were completely gone. A burden lifted. The glove I'd seen with the orange stripe did not belong to me. I was confident I was not the actor in some parallel existence. Relief washed over me.

As I left Georgina's office and no longer felt like I'd been dropped into a scene from Daphne du Maurier's *Rebecca*, it suddenly seemed preposterous that I'd flooded my thoughts with the possibility I'd murdered someone in another universe. Just because my life was *The Twilight Zone*, and I spoke to ghosts and had a twin who most people couldn't see, didn't mean my dreams were real-life events. It was a dream—a random, albeit macabre, synaptic occurrence that had no more truth to it than the dream I'd had last week that my cat Oreo could fly. True, he had the leaping capacity of a cougar, but so far he hadn't sprouted wings.

I slipped into my truck and headed back to my café, Break Thyme. It wasn't far, about ten minutes. Georgina's office was on the other side of the Malia River, which ran through Bookend Bay. I used to own a house on the river, but thankfully it had sold last summer. I'd worried it would never sell and would always be known as the house where my tenant was murdered. Geez, no wonder I was dreaming of murder. Thanks to a newspaper article in the Bookend Bay Bugle, even the townsfolk were starting to call me and my best friend Toni the Murder Gals, an epithet we didn't appreciate, even if we'd brought a few murderers to justice. Who wanted to be known as a Murder Gal? Maybe that moniker, having worked its way into my subconscious, was responsible for my dream.

Having been a homeowner for twenty-five years, selling the house had been freeing in ways I'd not expected. I no longer worried if I could afford to re-shingle the roof over my head. Yard maintenance was inconsequential. My energy costs had decreased drastically—mainly because I'd lived in my recreational vehicle, Longfellow, last summer. But the trailer wasn't winterized.

Break Thyme had done so well since I'd opened it two and half years ago that I'd renovated the second floor of my café into a small apartment where I'd spent the winter. Ray, my contractor, put up walls to give me a living and bedroom space. Break Thyme's kitchen was a decent size and completely functional, so I used that to cook my meals. But as convenient as it was living at Break Thyme, I planned to move back into Longfellow for the summer to take advantage of a lakeside view.

I pulled into a parking spot in Moose Harbor, locked the truck, and took the boardwalk to the back entrance of the café. Unlike my hypnotic dream, there was no impending gale. The lapping waters of the majestic Lake Superior were brilliant blue and reflected white puffs of clouds so bright my eyes hurt, making me regret I'd left my sunglasses in the truck.

I waved to Olivia and Henrietta, sitting on a bench in Courtesy Park. Olivia co-owned Ollie's Outfits with her twin brother and Henrietta had the bakery. If I hadn't been away from my café for the last two hours, I'd have wandered over to catch up, but I wanted to get to work.

The aroma of our Glazed Strawberry Almond Scones met me as I entered the kitchen. *Yum.* I loved that the café smelled like whatever baked goods we featured that month. A dozen scones sat cooling on a rack. It looked as if Toni had just baked another batch, meaning we'd likely sold out. Our June scones were proving to be extra popular.

I hung my coat in the closet and grabbed my apron as Toni came into the kitchen carrying a pastry plate.

"Hey," she said. "How was your session?"

"Revealing. I'm glad I went. I feel much better and think I can put the dream behind me now." I didn't want to go into details in case someone overheard us. Besides Toni, no one else at Break Thyme knew I talked to dead people and had a twin from a parallel world. It had seemed prudent to keep those aspects of my weird life on the down low.

"Glad to hear it." Toni set the plate on the counter, moved closer to me, and lowered her voice. "And for the record, I didn't think for one minute you'd been involved in a murder in this world or any other."

"Thank you for that vote of confidence, but don't you think everyone has the capacity to kill, given the circumstance?" I lowered my voice, too. "What if I'd been in a fight for my life? Or in a fight for someone else's life? One of my kids? Or you?"

"Do you think that's what happened?"

Not after I'd walked the beach, found that glove, and not seen the victim or the murderer. "No, I don't. Now, I think it was just a random dream, albeit a vivid one."

"Well, don't have any more murder dreams, okay?" Toni said, picking up tongs.

"Yes, Ma'am. How's everything been here?"

"We've had more customers than usual, which gave the Luddites something to complain about when we ran out of scones, so I whipped up another batch."

The Luddites were regulars at Break Thyme, a group of self-named retired men who longed for the good old days. "You are amazing. I probably would have told them tough luck."

"I nearly did, but then I realized it gave me an excuse to take a break from you know who," Toni whispered.

I closed the door between the kitchen and the café. "Oh, dear. What did she do now?" I'd hired Ivy last fall when my summer staff left at the end of the season. One thing about small-town living was that the potential employee pool was also small. Ivy was competent, but her strong personality rubbed Toni the wrong way, especially since Ivy was only nineteen years old and knew everything under the sun. Thankfully, I still had Poppy, my star employee who was on vacation in Bermuda with her boyfriend, Deputy Cody Wilson.

Ivy's laughter drifted into the kitchen through the door. I couldn't complain about her rapport with the customers. Most of the townsfolk had known Ivy's family for decades and took her precocious airs with a grain of salt.

"She tried to tell me how to cut in my butter the *proper* way," Toni said, rolling her eyes. "As if I hadn't been baking since before she was a thought, and I needed guidance from a kid."

I laughed at the nerve of Ivy giving baking advice to Toni, who, short of Henrietta, was the best baker I knew. "One day, she'll look back on these years and realize she still had a few things to learn about life."

"I'd love to be around to see that." Toni finished filling the pastry plate, and I went up front to check on things.

"You're back," said Ivy, looking a little disappointed. Hmm, maybe she preferred not having the boss around. She continued emptying the dishwasher with one hand and swiping mugs dry with the other. No one could complain about her efficiency.

"Everything good?" I asked.

"Of course. It's all under control. I'm moving all the mugs to the right side of the coffeemaker, though. It makes more sense, don't you think, since we're all right-handed here?"

"Okay." I wasn't sure if it made more sense, but I wasn't an anal person, unlike my OCD invisible twin.

"That's not going to help," came Brielle's voice behind me. Speak of the devil. "If you pour the coffee with your right hand, then the mugs should be on the left side where they've always been."

Ah, finally, she was gracing me with her presence. I might think I'd conjured her with my thoughts, but that couldn't be true since I'd thought of her a lot lately. I was eager to talk, wanting to know where she'd been for the last three weeks. By her expression, I could see something had changed.

"Let's leave the mugs on the left, Ivy," I said. "I'll be upstairs if you need me."

Chapter Two

I CONGRATULATED MYSELF FOR not being startled by Brielle's sudden appearance. Finally, I was getting used to her popping into my life when I was in a public place. I didn't want to react when she was invisible to everyone else, so I just bounded up the stairs, knowing she'd follow.

Brielle visited my life when she was sleeping in hers. Luckily, we had different sleep schedules. She usually turned in earlier than I did, and since she lived in England, the time difference between us meant I was often still awake when she dream-traveled into my life. Often, but not always.

Sometimes, we didn't connect, but I'd see signs of her visits when I woke. A compulsive clean freak, she had my café and trailer sparkling. Or putting her artistic skills to work, she occasionally left me a sketch or a painting. Not to sound like I was taking advantage, but I liked our arrangement and didn't want it to end. Not because of the free maid service, but because I'd grown fond of Brielle. We knew each other in ways no one else ever would.

Every day that passed with no sign of her, and there had been twelve days this time, had me worrying her ability to visit me could end as abruptly as it had started. Who knew how these parallel universe crossings worked? I couldn't even begin to understand the physics of parallel worlds. Sometimes I pictured her stepping into my life through a split in a curtain between dimensions.

Maybe our disconnect had somehow prompted my dream, although I could only speculate about this and didn't know what good that would do.

Eager to know what had been going on with her lately, I ran up the stairs and closed the door behind her.

"It seems like it's been ages since we've talked. Where have you been? Are you okay?" As I asked these questions, I realized whatever was going on, it hadn't worried her like it had me. She looked calm as could be. And happy. And refreshed, but then again, she usually did. Her off-the-shoulder print ruffle dress made her look lovely and feminine. Her skin glowed and her hair looked professionally tousled, as if that was a thing.

Glancing down at my polyester sweater, I considered it might have seen too many wash cycles. Just because my apron hid most of my sweater didn't mean I should wear it to work, but often I threw on whatever was coziest. During the decades when my focus had been on raising a family, Brielle, who'd been childless, seemed to have gained mad skills in fashion and cosmetology, talents that escaped me. Or maybe, when it came down to it, I just didn't care enough to prioritize these things. It was time to accept my pedestrian style and stop comparing myself to an alternate me I was never meant to be—as soon as I got my head around that reality.

To my credit, though, I did have a little something to be proud of. Over the last five months, I'd lost ten pounds using an exercise and calorie-counter app. And it hadn't been all that difficult, either. As long as I walked for forty-five minutes every day and kept track of my caloric intake, I could still have a treat and keep to my weight-loss plan.

Brielle lifted her hands into the air and smiled widely. "I'm more than okay, Quinn. I'm in love."

This was a surprise. "I didn't know you were seeing someone." She'd never talked about pursuing a relationship, more to the contrary. She loved being single since her job as an authors' assistant often had her traveling.

She sighed happily. "I met Julien when I was in Avignon last year on tour. He's a French author and was a guest speaker at the Provence Book Festival. We had a lovely afternoon over a bottle of Bordeaux, but then I went on to Prague and didn't hear from him until a couple of months ago."

Avignon. Prague. Well, la-di-da. "Really? What did the French author have to say?"

Her eyes turned dreamy. "Well, he reached out to me professionally, asking for my assistance. He's written a new book and wanted help with the launch next month."

A new author to add to her roster. Probably a famous, best-selling, hot one. Just the thought of a man with a French accent...I tried not to sigh. "Congratulations," I said, smiling to tamp down my envy. I really was happy for her. "That's exciting. What does he write?"

"Fantasy with wizards and warfare. Incredibly creative with complex plots and well-developed characters. He's a brilliant writer. His first book was a sensation and made all the best-seller lists. I'm going to work hard to ensure his second book does even better."

"With you on his team, I'm sure it will." I meant that. Despite our differences—and we did have them since our lives took separate directions at the age of eighteen—we were fundamentally the same person with traits in common, so I knew she'd work hard to achieve whatever goal she set for herself and her clients.

She flopped into my new lounge chair and swung her feet up onto the footstool. "I've never felt like this before. Right now, I've got this image in my head of Julien's eyes—dark, inescapable pools that...oh, Quinn. When he looks at me, it's like, I don't know how to describe it, all-encompassing. The world melts away—it really does—and there's nothing but the two of us in those moments. I'm so willingly adrift in Julien. I've hardly slept a wink in the past two weeks." Her dreamy gaze floated over the room, landing on mine.

"And he cooks," she continued. "He makes a vichyssoise to die for, and he knows how to pair wines to bring out the subtlest flavors. Always local because no one does wine like the French. And the cheese! We had a Brie de Meaux for breakfast that we picked up at the most delightful market. He fed me cherries, Quinn! Dangled them over my lips. It was one of the most sensual experiences of my life until I had to spit out the pit." She laughed.

I laughed, too. I'd never seen her so animated. "I'm really happy for you. Are you planning to stay in France?"

"I don't know. It's too soon, isn't it? I can't make a decision like that, not yet. Oh, I wish you could smell this man. He wears a cologne I could breathe all day."

I laughed at the thought of meeting him and taking a whiff, not that I could meet him. "I'll leave the smelling to you."

"You know, I was happy on my own, but I can't begin to describe how wonderful it is to be with Julien. He's curious about everything—which I love. He's thoughtful, supportive, and smart as a whip."

"He sounds perfect, and I can see how happy you are."

She leaned forward, knees knocking together. "I wish you could meet a man just like him. Maybe I'll make that my mission—to help you find true love. Oh! Wait. What about the park ranger? I've seen a spark in your eye when you talk about him."

I'd had a few really nice dinner dates with Alec Camden over the last nine months, but then weeks passed in between without us connecting. We certainly weren't having a whirlwind romance like Brielle and Julien—no cherries to be had. I couldn't blame him. I'd insisted I wasn't ready for anything beyond a friendship, and he respected that. But listening to Brielle and seeing the life in her eyes did make me envious. Falling in love was such a distant memory for me. I didn't think about it enough to value the experience and seek it out. "It's not that I've turned my back on love forever, but I need to be on my own to get to know myself again without my ex and my kids underfoot. I don't want to change my life. If it's not broken, don't fix it, right? Besides, with my café, I can barely keep up as it is. Where would I find time for a man?"

Her gaze narrowed on me. "That's not true, not at all. Where would you find time? Well, hello—wasn't it just winter? Wouldn't it have been nice to have Alec keep you warm since you won't leave Bookend Bay and go south like a civilized person? Break Thyme isn't that busy yet. And it's not as if you're knee deep in another investigation. What's keeping you so busy?"

How'd she get to be so direct? And as far as investigations went, I'd been looking forward to talking to her about my dream. Forget that. She wouldn't be able to stop talking about Julien long enough, anyway. I *was* happy for her newfound romance, but I didn't appreciate her saying I should just have up and left Break Thyme for the winter. My life was *not* lacking because I didn't have a Julien. "Well, I did renovate this space, so I had somewhere to live, and I do need to keep my business going. Not just to pay for the roof over my head, but because I love my café."

She looked around, finally registering her surroundings to take in the final renovation and my new furniture. "Oh gosh! I'm sorry. I didn't even notice. Can you believe it? Talk about being distracted." She got up and turned a full circle. "It was smart to expose that brickwork. And this turquoise chair gives a nice pop of color." She touched the faux fur blanket on the back of the chair. "It's really cozy in here."

Cozy, meaning it's not the South of France. "Thank you. I like cozy."

"I know you do."

A knock sounded at the door.

"Just a sec. On the phone," I called, latching onto my usual excuse to explain my conversation.

"Okay," Ivy called through the door. "I have a message for you."

I grabbed my cell phone and held it as I opened the door. "Yes?"

"There's a friend of yours downstairs. Nell Reynolds, and she'd like to speak with you when you have a chance."

Nell was a high school friend of mine, one I didn't get to see often enough, who'd moved away years ago to live in Marquette near her son. "Okay. Tell her I'll be right there. I'll just finish up my call."

"Kk," she said, as she did lately, ever since I'd responded *okay* to a text she'd written me. My response had offended her. She'd asked why I was being so passive aggressive. Since when had *okay* become passive-aggressive? Try as I might, I could not keep up with these kids.

"Quinn, I'm sorry if I've been going on and on about Julien," Brielle said when I closed the door. "I know I sound like a teenager in love for the first time." She sighed. "I really do want you to have the same happiness. We've both been through divorces, and well, I never told you about my marriage and why it ended. Maybe you'll understand when I do."

I was definitely intrigued but didn't think this was a story to tell in a hurry. "I'd love to hear about it, but a friend is waiting downstairs."

"I know. I heard. We'll talk next time."

"Enjoy every minute of your time with Julien."

"I will and thank you. I'll stay up here, so I won't distract you." She blew me a kiss and walked toward my desk, where she'd find something to tidy up. I had to admit a few times I put off dusting because I knew she'd do it. Neither of us were comfortable sitting idle, and she'd be here until she woke up in her own life or stopped dreaming, I guess.

Downstairs, I found Nell sitting in the Cozy Nook with a spiced gingerbread coffee. From the crumbs left on the plate, it looked like she'd polished off the ginger biscotti cookie we served with the coffee.

"Hello, my friend," she said, getting up to give me a hug. I didn't know if her hair color was natural, but it had been white for at least a decade. The short pixie cut looked fabulous on her. When I sat, I noticed dark circles under her eyes.

"It's great to see you, Nell. It's got to have been two years since we last saw each other."

"Two and a half. I came for your opening, but you were so busy that day we didn't get to talk. Before that, I'm not sure when we last saw each other. It has to be years. I don't get into Bookend Bay as often as I'd like."

"Every day, I'm more surprised by how quickly time passes," I said.

"I hear you. And on that note, do you have a few minutes?" she asked. "I should have called ahead, but I've got a busy work project that's taking all my energy. I'm sorry to tell you I have some bad news."

"Oh no. What's happened?"

"You remember Alicia Smallwood, from high school. She had an accident. A fatal one. She's dead." The words fell out, choppy and rushed.

I stared at Nell, slowly registering this news. As teenagers, Alicia, Nell, and I had hung out together, but Alicia and I never hit it off. She'd always been more Nell's friend and wasn't very nice to me when Nell wasn't around. After high school, they'd gone to the same college and had remained friends.

"That's sad to hear. I'm sorry, Nell." I took her hand and squeezed gently.

As a teenager, Alicia wasn't my favorite person, but people do grow, mature, and change. At least most people did. A few months ago, I'd run into her at the grocery store. I was in the checkout behind her. When she turned and I realized who it was, I smiled and said a friendly hello and something like *long-time, no see*, thinking it would be nice to catch up since I hadn't seen her in a decade. She made a sound that might have been a greeting, but then she'd looked away, like I wasn't worthy of her acknowledgment. At first, I'd been hurt, but I wasn't a kid any longer. Wiser now, I didn't judge Alicia. I didn't know what was going in her life or in her head. Maybe she had a demon or two in there.

"What happened to her?" I asked.

Nell's face sagged. "She drowned in the lake. The coroner said it occurred in the early morning—Sunday morning. That makes sense because she was religious about her rowing—went out every morning to keep in shape. Unless the forecast was ominous. She always checked first. That's what doesn't make sense. Alicia was afraid of bad weather."

Drowned? Like in my murder-dream? Goosebumps rose everywhere on my body, even between my toes. Was the victim in my dream Alicia? Not necessarily.

Don't panic. Unfortunately, accidents happened. People did drown. Last year, ninety-eight people were lost on the Great Lakes—I'd looked it up when my daughter went off with friends on a sailboat.

"Are you okay, Quinn?" Nell questioned. "You have a funny look on your face."

I wiped my damp palms on my pant legs. "Yes. I was just thinking it's sensible to be afraid of bad weather, especially on Lake Superior, which we all know can turn on a dime."

"Exactly. Everyone knows that." Nell let out a long breath. "The sheriff thinks Alicia was distracted and wasn't paying attention to the weather. They think it was an accident, but I'm not convinced, and it's eating me up inside."

I had no idea Nell and Alicia were that close. "If you don't think it was an accident, then what do you think happened?"

Nell clasped her hands together in her lap. "I think she rubbed someone the wrong way. You know, sometimes a person's strength can be their weakness, too. Alicia had an uncanny knack for seeing people, really seeing them. She was always up front with everyone and told it like she saw it. You never had to wonder what she was thinking."

That she rubbed someone the wrong way didn't surprise me, but I was astonished to learn she had uncanny people skills. But then again, I'd not been exposed to her positive attributes. I folded my arms across my chest against a sudden chill. Before I started thinking about who or why someone wanted Alicia dead, I wanted to know more about her.

"Did she have a family, Nell?"

Nell shook her head. "No. She had no one. Her parents passed years ago. She was married to the business."

"What business was she in?" I asked.

"We own Heart To Heart, a professional matchmaking service. We run it...I mean, ran it together."

Nell was in business with Alicia? Nell used to be a tax manager. "You do? How did I not know this?"

She sighed. "I guess that's my fault. I shouldn't have let so much time pass without getting in touch."

"It's not your fault. We've both been busy. It happens." She probably didn't know I was divorced. "So, you're in the matchmaking business. *That* is a surprise."

"If I'd had to do one more tax return, I was going to vomit." She chuckled. "One night, I was sitting with my husband, and I realized I'd matched five couples that year. It's like I have a sixth sense about it. When I meet a single person, I just know who they should be with, and nothing gives me more satisfaction than when the relationship works out. Alicia and I went to the Matchmaking Institute to learn the ropes. We started Heart to Heart six years ago. I absolutely love it."

Who knew there was a Matchmaking Institute? I scoffed a bit, feeling able to put my dream on the back-burner for now. There was nothing concrete to conclude Alicia's accident and my dream were connected. "You have a genuine love of people, but honestly, it's hard to picture Alicia as Cupid."

Nell smiled at that. "Oh, Alicia has skills. She's a good debater, and that's valuable as a matchmaker. People come to us with long lists of what they're looking for in a partner, and if necessary, Alicia tells them straight up why their ideals are not attainable or will take them down the wrong road." She shook her head. "Listen to me, talking about her in the present tense, as if she's still with us."

"I'm sure that's natural." Since I hadn't seen Nell in years, and I'd never been a fan of Alicia—rest in peace—I wondered why Nell had sought me out, although I had some idea. My reputation as one of the Murder Gals must have reached her. Toni and I had been approached by strangers who wanted us to spy on their spouses or discover family secrets, as if we'd hung out a Ladies Detective shingle, but we'd only joked about doing that, We'd agreed that if we could right a wrong, we'd do it, and with Brielle's help, we had a leg up. But so far, nothing implied Alicia hadn't died accidentally. Was there any evidence, other than a weather warning, to suggest someone had killed her?

"Was Alicia married?" I asked, wondering if a spouse might have had a motive for murder.

"Not married, but she'd been in a relationship recently with a man named Lennox Huff. That's why I'm suspicious. When she broke up with him, he took it badly. I know this because I walked in on an argument between them. He accused her of using him and said she'd be sorry for it. I thought that sounded like a threat, but she didn't take it seriously. She even let him enter our grand matchmaking event as a contestant. He said he was moving on, but I was skeptical. I think he was trying to make Alicia jealous by getting involved with someone else right in front of her. My intuition is telling me that Lennox is hiding something. He might have a dark side." She leaned forward. "Quinn, I'm here because I want to do you a favor."

Chapter Three

A FAVOR? THAT WAS a surprise. I'd thought she was going to ask me to investigate Alicia's death. "What kind of favor, Nell?"

"I heard about you and Bryan, that you've gotten a divorce. I was sorry to hear it. How are you?"

I brightened because my divorce had put me in a happier place. "I'm fantastic. Really. I know you have a good marriage, so you may not be able to relate, but Bryan and I had grown apart to the point where we no longer had the same interests or aspirations. We were bickering all the time. The divorce was freeing and enlightening. I hadn't realized how unhappy I'd become."

She smiled. "Well then, I'm happy for you. You've certainly made a success of Break Thyme."

"Thanks, Nell. I've worked twice as hard because Bryan believed my café would fail. No way I was letting him say, told you so."

"Of course not. The bum. So, do you see yourself in another relationship at some point? I'm not saying you need a relationship to be happy, and after a divorce you need time to be on your own, but in my line of work, I can't help but ask."

First Brielle and now Nell. "Sure, a little romance might be nice at some point, but I'm in no rush."

"Okay, this is where I can help."

"I don't think so, Nell. The thought of a dating service makes me uncomfortable."

"And why is that?"

I'd identified the roadblocks getting in my way because Toni and I had talked about using a dating site although it had just been talk. "For one, filling in a profile sounds like writing an advertisement which I'm horrible at. I'm not a good writer and can't imagine summarizing myself in a few paragraphs. I also can't imagine choosing a man based on a photo and a few paragraphs. Does everyone just choose the most physically attractive people? What if he's a great guy who doesn't know how to sell himself? I'd need to spend time with a man to know if we'd be a good fit. Besides, I don't understand what swiping left or right means."

Nell smiled. "That's why we started Heart to Heart. There's no swiping. We're not a dating app. We do a lot more than have our clients fill in a profile. The truth is, I'd like to help you get your feet wet in the dating world, not just because we're friends, and I want to see you happy. I imagine you'd see through that, considering my timing. I'm suggesting an exchange of favors."

"You want me to look into Alicia's death?"

"See how quickly you figured that out? I knew you're the best person for the job."

I rolled my eyes. "I'm not a professional, you know. I'm just curious and persistent enough to keep digging when things don't add up. I'm motivated by a good puzzle, but I have to be convinced there's been an injustice."

She scoffed. "You're being modest. I told you I'd heard about your divorce, well that's because I went to our high school reunion last spring. You know how everyone gossips. People want to know everything about everyone, and you were a hot topic...Murder Gal."

I groaned. "Not my favorite moniker."

"Then I won't use it again, but I meant what I said about helping you get comfortable dating. You can take it as slow as you want. Just have some fun with it. And your friend Toni, too. If you'll attend my matchmaking event and do a little nosing around to see if you think there's any merit to my concern about Alicia's death, I'll give you and Toni the royal treatment. I'm serious when I say Alicia had no life outside of work, so whoever did this to her had to be related to the business. I can't sleep thinking I may have a murderer nearby."

"Or not. That remains to be seen." I thought about it for a moment. Considering Break Thyme wasn't too busy, I could spare some time. "The royal treatment, huh? That doesn't sound too hard to take, but I have no idea what happens at a matchmaking event."

Nell leaned back, looking more relaxed. "Oh, well, you're going to love it. The event is taking place at Great Bear Resort, and we're pulling out all the stops. There's an indoor pool with a swim-up bar, a spa, and a golf course. You and Toni won't pay a cent. And hopefully finding true love will be the worst thing to happen." She gave me a look that took me back to the days when she used to goad me into stopping at the bakery for chocolate eclairs on the way home from school.

It was hard to argue against the royal treatment at Great Bear Resort, yet I was skeptical about the true love part. Also, I didn't want to feel obliged concerning Alicia's murder. "I can't make any promises, Nell, but I'll talk to Toni about it, and let you know."

Nell gave a sigh, then averted her gaze. "Thank you. I apologize for the short notice, but the event is happening this weekend, so as soon as you know…"

"I'll send you a text tomorrow."

She picked up her phone. "One more thing. I want to show you a photo of Lennox, so you know who he is." After some scrolling, she handed me the phone. "Alicia sent me that photo of the two of them. It was taken last summer."

They were standing on a beach. Alicia's hand was up by her face, as if she'd just moved a strand of her caramel-colored hair. She looked tanned. Happy. Her other hand was held by the smiling man beside her. A nice-looking man with thick, salt and pepper hair brushed back, revealing a forehead that had taken some sun. His eyes looked friendly behind black-framed glasses.

"They both look happy there," I said. It occurred to me that a matchmaker would probably date the cream of the crop since she had access to so many potentials.

"She *was* happy. I don't know what prompted their breakup. It seemed things between them were getting better every day, that Alicia had finally met her match, so to speak. He wasn't at all cowed by her, like some men. Now, I think perhaps he understated his strength and always had the upper hand."

I was about to give the camera back when I saw something on the ground behind them. A white rowboat with wood trim. I'd seen that boat recently. Goosebumps crawled over my skin. It looked like the same boat I'd seen in the hypnosis session.

"What's wrong?" asked Nell. "You've gone pale."

"Is that Alicia's boat?" I handed her the phone.

"Yes, that was her boat. She and Lennox had been out on the lake that day. I think they'd been fishing. She'd teased him about taking advantage of her rowing sessions to catch dinner. Why?"

I hesitated, wishing I was comfortable talking about my paranormal life, but it was bad enough being known as a Murder Gal. What would people say if they knew about Brielle or the ghosts who visited me? But this was Nell. A friend who'd played with Ouija boards and told ghost stories. Yet, if I told her about my dream and that the person had been murdered, should I also tell her about Brielle and my fear that somehow, I'd dream-traveled to the moment of Alicia's murder? I still didn't know the identity of my dream victim, or even if they'd survived. I didn't know if the whole thing was a figment of my imagination or if the dream was a psychic vision. Looking into Alicia's death might help me figure it out.

"No reason other than that being the boat that must have capsized," I said, keeping my weirdness to myself for now.

Nell nodded. "Yes, that's the one." She grabbed her purse from the floor. "I've got to get going. It's been really good seeing you. Let's have a proper visit when the event is over."

"I'd like that, and I promise to text you as soon as I talk to Toni." We said goodbye. As she headed out the patio door, I picked up her dishes and took them into the kitchen.

Toni was adding something to the shopping list on the fridge. "We're getting dangerously low on cinnamon. Wasn't that supposed to come in with the shipment yesterday?"

"Yes, it was. But now that you mention it, I don't remember seeing cinnamon. I'll run out and get some from the Horn of Plenty."

Toni snapped the dry erase marker into its holder. "Did I see you talking to Nell in the Cozy Nook?"

"Yes. It must be a long time since you've seen her."

"We chatted for a couple of minutes at your opening. So, did you have a nice visit?"

"It was nice to see her, but she wasn't in the best spirits. A friend of hers has died—Alicia Smallwood. I don't think you ever met Alicia. She and Nell were in business together."

"The name's not familiar."

"Nell thinks Alicia's death wasn't an accident. She drowned in the lake."

"Drowned? Quinn, is there any reason to think this is related to your dream?"

"Yes, I do think that." Of course, Toni knew about my dream. I'd go nuts if I didn't have her to confide in. She'd suggested I see the hypnotist. "Nell showed me a photo of Alicia's boat, and I'm sure it was the same boat I saw in my dream. She suspects Alicia's jilted boyfriend or even one of her employees."

"What do you think?"

"I think I need to look into it because of that dream," I said.

"Mm-hmm," Toni said. "If the boat is real, do you think the glove you saw in the bush is real, too?"

How did that slip my mind? "It's a good thing I'm not trying to do any of this on my own. Sometimes I think I need a team to manage my life."

Toni laughed. "I wouldn't want to manage *your* life alone. So, you verify where they found Alicia's boat, and we'll go check out the area. It's a good thing Poppy will be back tomorrow to look after things here, so we can spare some time."

Poppy was our biggest fan when it came to our mystery solving. Since she was dating Cody, a local deputy, and Cody seemed to respect our detecting skills, we occasionally shared details.

"Yes, it is, because this investigation comes with a few perks." I told Toni about the matchmaking event. Since her husband Norman died suddenly twelve years ago, she'd shown no interest in dating except for a short stint with a firefighter last year. But that experience seemed to prove to her she wasn't ready for a relationship. She'd put Norman on such a high pedestal, no man stood a chance, so she was going to work on that. But then she'd thrown herself into baking for Break Thyme and hadn't mentioned dating since. There was a good chance she'd hate the idea of this matchmaking event. I held my breath and waited for her reaction.

Chapter Four

"SIGN ME UP," SHE said, with no hesitation. "It sounds like a hoot. And who knows, maybe we'll have a little fun on the side."

Wow. Must be time to move forward. "I like your attitude. Let's make a point to have some fun with this."

"Bathroom break!" Ivy called from the front.

I cringed, not because I begrudged Ivy a break, but I hoped there wasn't a customer sitting at the counter to hear that.

"Just a sec," I said to Toni and stepped out front to see Ivy heading into the Nook for the bathroom. Three locals sat in a booth, but they were deep in conversation. The bells jingled over the front door. My heart melted when I saw who it was.

Hurrying to the front, I propped the door open for my daughter-in-law Chelsea to get the stroller inside. "You came to see Grammy!" I said, leaning down to take in my two-month-old grandson Gabriel's smile as he batted his arms in the air. People talked about how special it was to be a grandparent, but I couldn't have comprehended the profound love and joy this sweet baby brought into my world.

My relationship with my once self-centered daughter-in-law had improved immensely over the last six months, and I owed some of that to Brielle and much of it to motherhood. There was nothing like being a mother to take the attention from oneself. Brielle had opened my eyes to the role Chelsea's immature mother had played in fueling her daughter's princess complex. When I'd asked Chelsea for help with Break Thyme's social media platforms, she'd jumped at the chance to be helpful, and I started to see what a bright, creative young woman she was, qualities my son talked about but had eluded me. She was also an attentive mother to Gabriel. I didn't know what I would have done if Chelsea hadn't risen to the demands of her newborn and instead had expected my son Jordan to take the bulk of the workload. She'd even managed to get dinners on the table, which was another accomplishment.

"He saw a photo of you on my phone and got so excited, I had to bring him over," Chelsea said.

I wasn't sure he'd registered a phone photo, but I appreciated the sentiment. "You are both sweethearts." My heart was mush as I lifted Gabriel into my arms. He gurgled and stuffed his fist into his mouth. "Hello, my love," I said, nuzzling his neck. Mmm, baby smell.

"Do I hear a baby?" Toni came to give Gabriel a kiss on his forehead. "He smells so good. There's nothing like the scent of a baby. Someone should bottle it."

"I was just thinking that," I said.

"I can't stay long," said Chelsea. "I've got to get home and get Gabby to bed, but I wanted to show you the new graphic for next month's verb."

Our verb of the month was an original idea for a café. It had come about from a communications error. I'd asked an artist to paint an *herb* of the month sign over our menu, but she'd heard the word *verb*. When the sign was complete, I learned our customers loved playing along, so we'd kept the theme going.

"You do such a nice job with those images," Toni said, looking over Chelsea's shoulder.

I used a tissue from my pocket to wipe drool from Gabriel's chin and scooted over to the shelf behind the counter to grab a giraffe from the basket of toys I kept for him. It was times like this when I thoroughly appreciated owning my own business. Having baby toys on hand and taking a few minutes to play with my grandson at the end of the day were wonderful perks.

Now that Gabriel was happily chomping on the neck of the giraffe, I joined Chelsea and Toni, who were looking at the new design on Chelsea's iPad.

"Warning: Biting into June's scone of the month can make your eyes glaze over as you get lost in deliciousness. Stay tuned for more details," I read from the graphic. The word glaze would be the new verb. Chelsea made it look as if the word glazed was iced. "It's perfect!"

She was beaming. "Good! I'm posting this on Tuesday and calling it Tuesday's Teaser. Then we'll do a reveal of the new scone on June 1st. I'll need a photo, Toni."

"You bet," Toni said. "I want to do one more test recipe to be sure I've got the right amount of maple syrup in the glaze, but there's no reason I can't have it done tomorrow, as long as your mother-in-law remembers to buy cinnamon."

"I will not forget," I said.

"Excellent." Chelsea stuffed her iPad into the diaper bag. "Gabby's going to be hungry and tired, so I must get him home before he blows a gasket 'cause he has to wait two minutes for his last feed."

My grandson was a cheerful baby, but like most babies, he wasn't patient.

"Are we a spoiled little boy already?" said Ivy, coming over from the Nook and tickling Gabriel under the chin. He pulled back, turning his head into my neck.

"A two-month-old isn't spoiled because he lets you know he's hungry," I said, and set Gabriel into the stroller. "Hunger is hunger. It's better for everyone not to get him riled up."

"I always fed my babies on demand," said Toni. "You never know when they're going through a growth spurt and need to eat more."

"Mm-hmm," said Ivy, skeptically. "I suspect he's got you wrapped around his baby finger."

That was rather uncalled for. Ivy may think she knows everything there is to know about life, but she had some growing up to do.

"You're a mother?" asked Chelsea as she stuffed the diaper bag into the basket.

Ivy made a face. "Gosh no. I have younger siblings and I used to babysit. Some things are common sense, right? But everyone has their own opinions."

Chelsea laughed. "Yeah, I'd had lots before I actually had a baby. I'm going to keep doing things my way since it's no fun getting him to settle down once he's upset. And I babysat a couple times, too. Motherhood is not that easy. See ya later, people."

After we said goodbye and had cleaned and locked up, I walked over to the Horn of Plenty Market to grab cinnamon for Toni and apricots for my breakfast.

Chelsea and I were on the same wavelength when it came to mothering, but Ivy's comment about spoiling hit a nerve. While Chelsea had grown considerably over the last year, in my opinion, she'd been a spoiled, entitled young woman. While I truly believed Gabriel was too young to be spoiled, I wondered if Chelsea might find it difficult not to give in to a child who throws temper-tantrums when he doesn't get his own way. She'd even admitted to using this tactic herself as a child. Then again, it was not my responsibility to parent Gabriel. *Remember that, Grammy.*

As I entered the store, my thoughts turned to the matchmaking event and the prospect of dating. Alec popped into my head. If I was going to date anyone, and the prospect of dating still didn't excite me all that much, I'd be comfortable with him. I liked Alec's company. He was interesting. I usually learned something from him, which was even more attractive to me than his good looks.

I slung a basket over my arm because it was rare for me to buy no more than the two things I'd come for. Proving that true, I grabbed a bag of flax seeds and hemp hearts along with the apricots. A loaf of olive bread caught my attention, and I couldn't resist grabbing a wedge of Camembert after Brielle had made it sound so good.

As I headed down the spice aisle, I pictured Alec feeding me cherries and me having a mouth full of pits. I was smiling when I saw the broken bottle. I stopped short. Oil pooled across the middle of the floor. Walnut oil, I could see from the label—a big bottle. What a waste. I loved walnut oil but rarely bought it because it was expensive. Someone could slip on this.

A woman with long silver hair was standing in front of the sugars. I didn't recognize her and figured she was probably a tourist. I didn't want her to slip.

"Be careful," I called over to her. "I'll get someone to clean that up."

She looked up and smiled, her high cheekbones popping. Her skin was milk white, her color probably accentuated by her black dress. She looked down at the floor, then along the shelves. She looked confused, then she nodded and grabbed a bag of coconut sugar. "Have a lovely day," she said and walked the other way.

Hmm, strange. I double checked to be sure I was in the spice aisle. Yep. The sign overhead said baking needs and spreads.

I didn't have to look far. I recognized teen-aged Joel, stacking cartons of lemonade into the fridge in the next aisle.

"Joel, you've got a broken bottle of oil in the baking aisle."

He made a face. "Really? Ugh. Why does it have to be oil? That stuff's brutal."

I was glad it wasn't my job to clean it up. "Yes, it is, and slippery, too."

"Okay, I'll grab a mop."

"Happy cleaning," I said, cheerfully. Then I decided to treat myself to one of those lemonades. I still had to grab cinnamon, so I backtracked to the spice aisle.

"What the—" There was no broken bottle of oil. I must have the wrong aisle. But wait. This was the spice aisle, but I didn't see any oils on the adjacent shelves. I stood there for a few moments, recalling the broken glass and the pool of oil. Could I have been in a different aisle? Grabbing a package of cinnamon, I walked to the end and saw Joel coming toward me with a bucket and mop.

"It must have been the next aisle over," I said.

We checked. No oil spills. "Okay, this is really strange. I'm pretty sure it was in the spice aisle. It was right in front of all the oils."

"We don't have oils in the spice aisle."

"You don't?" Why was I so confused about where the oil was? I'd been shopping at this store for years, but as I thought about it, I realized Joel was right. I guess I'd just assumed the bottle had fallen from the shelf because the oils and vinegars were all the way on the other side of the store. There was no way I'd walked that far to find him. Unless I was completely distracted with Alec on my mind. I supposed that could be it, yet I was feeling oddly discombobulated, maybe because Joel was staring at me.

"I'm sorry, Joel. I must be wrong. Let's go check the oil aisle. It must be there."

As we crossed the store, the wheeling bucket made a creaking sound. I looked down every aisle, finally reaching the oils.

There was nothing. Not one drop of oil or shard of glass. No one could have cleaned up a mess like that so fast. Joel shot me a puzzled look, followed by the worst—pity.

"I don't know what's going on," I said, bewildered. "I apologize again."

"Don't worry about it. Someone probably cleaned it up already."

"Sure," I said, not believing that for a second. "Thanks for your help. Have a good day."

As he steered the bucket away, I remembered the woman with the silver hair. She'd taken a bag of coconut sugar from the shelf. I *had* taken Joel to the right aisle.

I turned to leave and caught the faint scent of walnuts. At least I thought I smelled walnuts, unless I'd imagined that, too. I sniffed a few times but couldn't be sure. Walnut oil had a delicate scent, so it could be hard to discern.

I didn't say a word to the cashier as she warned of flurries in the forecast. "Snow in May! Of all the nerve," she said, shaking her head.

Someone cleaned up that mess, lickety split, I told myself as I headed to my son's house. That had to be it. I was distracted by the thought of dating and more time passed than I'd thought, and in that time someone cleaned up, just like Joel said. Otherwise, my grip on reality was loosening, and I couldn't accept that. I had important things to do, like to give my grandson a bath and read him bedtime stories. Tonight. And no illusions of pooling walnut oil were getting in the way of that.

Before dawn the next morning, Toni and I met at Break Thyme to bake scones for the day.

After sunrise, we drove about twenty minutes to the beach where Alicia was found.

Toni hiked her foot up onto a stump to re-tie her shoelace. "So, if we find the glove you saw in your dream, that would mean it wasn't just a dream. It was a psychic vision."

I wasn't as excited about that as Toni sounded. "I don't want to have psychic visions, especially murderous ones. How will I be able to tell a vision from a dream?" But as I asked that question, I realized there had been an unusual quality to the dream-vision. An intensity and permanence. It hadn't faded away. It remained in my head.

"I don't know, but you're not alone in this. I'm with you, as much as I can be. There's got to be a reason for everything that's happening to you, Quinn. You're meant to do good with these new abilities of yours, and I'm meant to help you with it. That's what I believe."

It made me feel better to have her support, but she could never truly understand what it was like to have these experiences. Sometimes I wished I could meet another person like me. "Thanks, Toni. You're a good friend."

I stepped over a fallen log and held back branches for us to pass. We were on a path that led to Lake Superior close to the club where Alicia had rowed from every day.

When we reached the beach, I stopped to look down the length of the cove. A strange sense of déjà vu swept over me as if I'd experienced this moment before—a good sign we were in the right place. The water was high, which was often the case in the spring, reducing the width of the beach.

"Let's go this way," I said, remembering that in my vision Alicia's boat had been in the middle of the cove. The wind blew my hair about my face, so I tucked it behind my ears.

Farther along, we passed a man throwing a stick into the water for his collie. We said hello and kept going. My gaze was fixed on the bushes for any sign of the glove or anything else out of the ordinary.

"There's a nice piece of driftwood," Toni said, bending over to pick up the worn smooth, knobby wood. Always thinking creatively.

A family of ducks gave us a wide berth as we tried to stay on dry land when the water came close to the grasses. There'd been grasses near the bush where I'd seen the glove. We'd come to the middle of the cove. I stopped walking and looked out over the water, scanning the horizon to the end of the cove where a long, tree-covered rocky point jutted out.

I'd seen that point in my vision. The same shape, like a finger, and the distance was similar from where I now stood. "Toni! I recognize that peninsula over there from my dream. If that glove was real, it should be in these bushes somewhere." I pointed at the greenery running along the beach. "The orange stripe stood out, so it should be easy to see."

"Okay, but it's been a few days, so the wind could have blown it elsewhere."

"That's true," I said, pulling gloves from my pocket. "It's odd to be looking for something you don't want to find." I lifted a low hanging cedar branch and peered underneath.

Toni gave a soft snort. "But finding it will make you even more special."

Now it was my turn to snort. "If you want to be president of my fan club, the position is available."

"Let's see if you can materialize that glove before I order buttons printed with your photo for your fans."

I caught the roar of a motorboat as I continued my search. If the glove had blown into the water, it could be gone forever, if it even existed. The wind carried the peaty smell of algae. I swatted away a deer fly and regretted not using bug spray.

The air turned cooler when a cloud blocked the sun and cast the shoreline into shadows. I hoped the diminished light wasn't enough to hide a flash of orange.

Thirty minutes later, I was reconsidering our finding the glove when a pop can blew down the beach. It always annoyed me when people disrespected our stunning natural environment with their litter. How difficult was it to take your garbage with you?

Toni and I chased after the can. She plucked it from the water and held it upside down to let any contents drain. "I'm starting to think it would be almost impossible for anything to stay put in this wind."

"I know. I've been having the same thought. The glove could have blown into the bushes, and from there it could easily have followed the route that soda can just took and was washed away, or it never existed in the first place."

"Just because we can't find it doesn't mean it doesn't exist," Toni said.

I didn't have a solid reason for my belief in the glove, just a feeling in my core, and I wanted to trust this. "The shoreline is the same as in my dream. Alicia's boat exists, and I saw it at the same time I saw the glove. So, I'm going to believe in the glove. It's just not going to be handed to us on a silver platter. We're going to have to work a little harder to solve this."

"Then that's what we're going to do. Shall we get to work?"

"Yep, let's put on our lipstick and get to the bottom of this matchmaking, dream-vision mystery."

Chapter Five

THREE DAYS LATER, ON Friday afternoon, I dropped off my cat Oreo at Jordan's house and got to spend a few minutes cuddling Gabriel.

While I was away at the matchmaking event, I could have left Oreo upstairs at Break Thyme because Poppy would give him lots of attention, but he and Gabriel had quickly formed a special bond. Since Jordan loved the cat, he'd offered to take him. Sometimes our cat could be grumpy, but when Gabriel got a fistful of fur, Oreo was gentle as a lamb and waited patiently for someone to rescue him.

After one last baby kiss, I said goodbye and picked up Toni. Great Bear resort was a forty-five-minute drive from Bookend Bay, so I'd be able to return to Break Thyme if they needed me. Home from her holiday, Poppy was refreshed and ready to get back to work. Capable and trustworthy, she'd never given me a reason to worry when the café was in her hands.

It was late afternoon by the time we arrived. After we drove through the gates, the road took us up a steep hill, where we caught sight of the lake and the resort sprawled across many acres. The main building looked like a massive three-story log cabin. From this height, I saw a dozen smaller cabins spaced along narrow roads running under a canopy of trees. I'd never vacationed here and was taken aback by how beautiful it was.

Toni and I hauled our bags from the back seat of my truck and walked toward the main building. My gaze was drawn to a bunch of huge, heart-shaped balloons tethered to the second-story balcony. Since it was unseasonably cold, fire pits filled the air with the smell of campfires. I loved that smoky scent. It reminded me of camping holidays and fun times. Around each fire sat Adirondack chairs and side tables. Laughter came from one group of women who appeared to be having drinks.

"Look at this place," Toni said as we entered the lobby through wooden doors that boasted an intricately carved scene featuring a bear and a moose. Inside, we stood gawking at the gorgeous wood and a ceiling that must have been forty-feet high. Spectacular Anishinaabe art adorned the walls and brought vibrant colors into the space. A huge stone sculpture of a grizzly bear and cubs sat off to the side. I drew in the woodsy, resinous scent. This place had all my favorite smells.

"We get to stay here for a week?" Toni said. "I don't think I'm going to want to leave."

"No kidding." I was feeling pretty lucky to have this resort experience, even if we planned to work. Who knew our investigative skills would bring perks like this?

"I guess we better check in," Toni said.

We crossed the lobby to the reception counter, a gleaming display of cedar. At least I guessed it was cedar from the scent.

"Looks like we go over there," I said, noticing a table at the end of the counter with a Heart to Heart logo on a sign. A brown-haired, big-boned woman with straight bangs, a cheerful smile, and a stunning suntan sat behind the table admitting a man to the event.

I listened as she leaned over a paper map explaining where he'd find his room, one that appeared to be in the resort itself. I was hoping Toni and I would get a cabin in the woods, but I certainly couldn't bemoan any mode of accommodation since Nell was footing our bill.

"Will you be paying by credit or debit?" the young woman asked the man ahead of us.

"Credit, please," he said, removing his wallet from his back pocket.

Toni gave him a sidelong glance and winked at me. From behind, the guy looked pretty good—his jeans hugged his butt nicely.

Why was I ogling a guy's butt? If I'd learned anything about life, butts were not a good indicator of decency, kindness, smarts, optimism or sense of humor—qualities I appreciated in Alec.

Seconds after the guy inserted his card he said, "It's not working."

"Oh, crap," said the dark-haired woman as she pushed buttons on the debit machine. "Not again. This thing always gives me a hard time." She handed the pin pad to the guy. "I'm sorry. Do you mind doing it over?"

"Not at all," he said, in a voice that reminded me of smooth whiskey.

Holy cow. I hadn't been here for five minutes, and I was already feeling warm. Darn hot flashes lived on. Wearing a coat indoors was too much warmth. I set down my bag and unzipped.

We waited while the guy tried again. And once more, to no avail.

The woman let out her breath in a huff, then smiled tightly. "I'll have to call for tech support, but I don't want to make you wait. Why don't you go up to your room and get settled in? Can you come back to try again before five, please?"

"Sure, no problem. Or you could take down my credit card details and input the charge when it's working."

"That would be great if you're okay with that. I promise to shred your credit card details afterward."

"Okay, we have a deal. You have a trustworthy face. Besides, it's not like I don't know who I gave my info to."

She made a clicking sound with her tongue. "True. Guess I can't get away with a couple of spa treatments, huh?" She said it with a grin and wrote down his numbers.

When he was done, he stuffed his wallet into his pocket and picked up the duffel at his feet. Turning, he glanced our way, gave a quick nod, and flashed gleaming white teeth in a smile. His gaze lingered on Toni as he walked past us.

"Ooh la la," Toni said when he was out of earshot.

I nudged her arm and approached the desk.

"I'll be with you in just one moment," the young woman said, looking stressed. "I need to call tech support."

"No problem. Take your time." Just being in this place for five minutes had me feeling more relaxed than I'd been in a long time.

Toni picked up a brochure from the table. "I could go for a massage. Do you find, now that you're single, you don't get your blood circulating like you used to? Norman gave great shoulder rubs and foot massages." She sighed.

Her deceased husband was a saint. My ex, not so much. "I can't remember ever getting a foot rub from Bryan."

"Well, we're going to find you a man who's going to change that," she said. "I'm thinking we need to do this kind of thing more often, minus the possible murder aspect."

I laughed. "Agree. Massage minus murder." Just the thought of a week in this place was sending sparks of joy through me.

The woman finished her phone call and stood. Her expression turned upbeat and enthusiastic as she extended her hand. "Welcome to Great Bear Resort and the Heart to Heart event. I'm Courtney. I'll be getting you registered today, and I'll be around throughout the event if you need anything or have questions."

"Nice to meet you. I'm Quinn Delaney, and this is Toni Miller."

"Ah. Our guests of honor. Nell told me to expect you both this evening. You'll be staying in one of the cabins. You're going to love it. They're really nice."

"Great!" said Toni. "We were hoping for one of those. What a beautiful place this is."

"I know," Courtney said. "Wait till you see the restaurants and the pool. There's also an art gallery. And by the way, all the artwork you see in the lodge is for sale."

"We can't wait to look around," I said, wishing I had the budget for art like this. I hadn't seen a piece under seven thousand dollars.

"Let me get your keycards, and I'll show you how to find your cabin," Courtney said. The diamond on her finger caught the light and sparkled as she rifled through a file folder. "Ah, here you are."

She set a sheaf of papers on the table with keycards paper-clipped to the top. "I'm going to need you to fill in these forms as soon as you can since everyone else filled them in weeks ago. If you could get them to me by 8 a.m. tomorrow, before the breakfast social, that would be helpful. We want to be sure you spend time with your best possible matches."

Her gaze caught on something behind us and a smile filled her attractive face. "Here comes tech!"

A young guy sauntered past us to join Courtney behind the desk. He looked at Toni and me and nodded. Then he seemed to do a double take and looked back at me. He stared for a moment and then looked away. *Why did he look at me like that? Was my face beet red?* I fanned myself with my hand.

"Problem with the debit machine, huh," he said. "Sorry about that. I'll get it fixed right away. Usually just have to give it a reboot."

"We're not waiting for the machine," Toni said. "At least I don't think so." She looked at Courtney questioningly. "Do we have to pay?"

"Nope, you're all good to go." Courtney beamed at the young man. "This is Dario, by the way. If you need any tech help while you're here, he's your guy. And he's my guy, too. My fiancée! I just love saying that word. Fiancée! It's a word we like to hear at Heart to Heart."

I laughed. "I guess so. You look happy, too. A true testament to Heart to Heart's matchmaking."

Dario smiled but didn't lift his head from the machine.

"It really is," Courtney said. "I only agreed to marry him because he's from Columbia, so we get to go south in the winter." She laughed. "Just kidding. I would have married him even without perks."

Dario chuckled. "Sure. She only loves me for my family."

"I'm not a winter person, so I'd consider your family a pretty nice bonus," Toni said, then looked at Courtney. "You look like you've been somewhere sunny. You have a great tan."

"Thank you. We've been back two weeks already, and I've still got good color. Dario took me to meet his family in Cartagena. Their place is amazing." She leaned forward and lowered her voice. "I think I hit the jackpot, but don't tell him I said so, or it'll go to his head." She was obviously teasing because he could hear her.

"I'm sure Dario believes he's hit the jackpot, too," I said. Courtney seemed like a vivacious, friendly young woman.

"Yeah, she's okay," he said in an equally teasing tone. *Ah, young love.*

Courtney swatted him.

The debit machine bleeped and printed something.

"It was actually Alicia's idea to set us up," she said, and then her expression turned solemn as if she'd just remembered Alicia was dead.

"I'm sorry for your loss," I said. "It must be difficult for everyone to carry on at full throttle, managing an event of this magnitude."

"Alicia would have wanted it that way. Everyone seems to be doing okay, though. I wasn't close to Alicia, but it's still sad."

Dario glanced at Courtney. His forehead wrinkled, then he made the sign of the cross. "Yeah, rest in peace, boss lady." He moved the machine closer to Courtney. "It should be working okay now."

"Phew," she said. "I hope so. I still have nightmares about that time we were using the machine outside, and I couldn't get it to work. It was so hot, people were melting. It was horrible."

I could relate to the stress of debit machine mishaps. We used one at Break Thyme and had had similar issues at times. "There's usually a support phone number right on the terminal, Courtney. If you're stuck again, just call them. They're pretty good at getting things working."

She looked down at the terminal. "What? Where?"

Dario crossed his arms over his chest, showing impressive biceps. "It's on the back, Court, but you can call me anytime." He winked at her.

Her eyes turned sultry as she bumped his hip with her shoulder. "I do prefer a visit from tech support."

Okay, now things were teetering on the edge of unprofessional and sending my thoughts into the bedroom, and I certainly didn't want to be in theirs. I cleared my throat. "On that note, we're going to get to our room. It was nice to meet you guys."

"You, too," Courtney said, her face slightly flushed.

Toni snatched our check-in papers from the table and was laughing under her breath as we left the main building. "We can find the cabin on our own. I think those two were getting distracted."

I laughed. "It did look that way." It was a relief to get outside and feel the crisp air on my face cooling me down. "I wonder if there's often an undertone of romance between employees when you work for a matchmaker?"

"Sounds like a nice perk to me. Maybe Heart to Heart doesn't attract employees determined to remain single."

"Maybe, but who knows? So, what's our cabin number?"

Toni slid her bag into the crook of her arm and checked the key cards. "Number 11." Bobbing her chin, she indicated the back of a cabin off the main road. "Shall we have a look at that one there and see what number it is?"

"Actually, let's drive," I suggested, feeling eager to put my feet up. "It looks like we'll have our own parking spot."

We walked past the fire pits to the parking lot, then drove along the side road to cabin 11, nestled among soft-wood trees and silver birch. Our homey quarters were L-shaped with a center deck leading to an eggshell blue front door with windows on either side.

"This is really nice," I said, anticipating it to be as lovely on the inside.

Toni opened the door. I wasn't disappointed. On the left, a stone wall housed a gas fireplace. Two red loveseats faced each other with a large ottoman in between and tartan blankets folded on top.

"We each have our own bedroom," Toni said, peeking into the rooms. "I wasn't expecting that, and there's chocolate on our pillows. How nice. Which room do you want?"

"I don't care. Take whatever one you prefer."

Toni dropped her bag inside one of the rooms. "I'm going to check out the bathroom."

"I'll be right behind you." My age seemed to be inversely related to my bladder size. I removed my shoes and grabbed my slippers from my bag. I loved slippers and couldn't wait to put on my pajamas. It was funny how my entertainment preferences had changed over the years. I wasn't alone in that. Toni and I had already discussed how we were both excited to open a bottle of wine, eat potato chips—I'd budgeted my calories to include the wine and fifteen chips—and watch old *I Love Lucy* episodes on our down time. I'd even brought an HDMI cord and a portable DVD player.

After we'd changed clothes and I'd opened the wine, Toni tossed me one of the packages Courtney had asked us to fill in. "I guess we'll have to do this paperwork if we want to blend in enough to figure out if Alicia's ex-boyfriend, or anyone else, wanted her dead. What was his name again?"

"Lennox Huff." I read the quote at the top of the page. "Singles who choose Heart to Heart are three times more likely to find a life partner than those who go it alone."

"Hmm," said Toni, leafing through the pages. "There are a lot of questions here. Wait. What's this?" She held up a sheet. "This is a release form for photographs and video." She read further, then looked at me. "Did you know this event is part of a competition to win a prime television special—Love After Forty? There's another matchmaking company in this competition called Cupid Connection."

"What? No. Nell didn't say anything about that." I leafed through my package to find the page Toni was reading. Sure enough, it looked like the desired outcome of this event was to generate as many potential love matches as possible.

"Whoever has the most love matches between Heart to Heart and Cupid Connection wins the television spot. That's when the filming starts, so we don't have to worry about that." Toni scanned the leaflet while I poured Shiraz into our wine glasses.

"Cheers to falling in love the old fashion way—without lights and cameras," I said.

"Or fame." Toni clinked my glass. "So then, after these two weeks at the resort, it looks like the couples in potential love matches get dropped off in a tropical location where the end goal is a wedding."

"What? Marriage?" I screwed up my face. "How long will these couples have known each other by then?"

"I don't know," Toni said, giving a soft snort. "They'll come home and meet each others' families, so maybe six weeks?"

"Good grief. How can you know a person well enough to marry them in that time? Some people hide their true colors like it's an art form. It's got to take at least two years to see all the sides of a person, don't you think?"

"Well, it sure takes more than a few weeks, although I knew I wanted to spend my life with Norman after our first date, and I wasn't wrong about him."

"You're a good judge of character. I imagine if any of these people have kids, they'll have something to say about impromptu marriages."

"That probably adds to the drama. More conflict means higher ratings. The producers probably don't care if the marriages end in divorce. Do you think people will do it just to be on television?"

"Yes, I bet you're right." Placing my wine glass on the table, I got up to grab the potato chips from the counter housing the coffeemaker. Hickory barbecue. My favorite. I opened the bag and offered them to Toni, who grabbed a handful.

After plopping down on the couch, I counted my chip allotment into a napkin.

The rest of the event package consisted of a profile questionnaire so Heart to Heart could match me with the man of my dreams. "Since the idea of being on a television romance show appeals to me as much as finding a nest of tarantulas in my coffee maker, I think I'll fudge my answers to these questions."

Toni laughed. "Now, you're talking, girl. Maybe we should finish this bottle of wine first. Might provide inspiration."

"Definitely." I took a healthy gulp. "It kind of bugs me that Nell didn't mention this competition."

"Sure, but maybe she's been distracted by the murder of her friend and business partner?" Toni arched an eyebrow.

"Maybe," I conceded. "I won't give her a hard time about it, but I'd gotten a little excited about the potential of meeting someone, and now I feel let down because there's no way I'm going to be part of a TV special. Don't you feel the same?"

"Yes," she admitted. "I surprised myself. This event got me thinking about the qualities of a man I might consider dating. Would I want a man with different interests that might expand my horizons or similar interests, so he'd feel familiar and safe?"

"Like a guy who watches TV oldies in his pajamas with wine and potato chips? Oh, and he should bake, too. You love your oven."

She laughed. "Exactly. I'm going to write that one down—a man who isn't afraid to get cozy and bake a mean scone."

Smiling, I picked up the questionnaire, gave it a scan, then grabbed a pen. "I know what you mean, though. I'm going to say I want the perfect blend of similar, yet different."

"Good point," she said. "I'm writing common yet novel."

"Perfect."

"It's not like we're looking for husbands," she said, then tossed back her wine.

"Not husband material." I wrote that on my form.

"What about kissing?" Toni said.

"I don't feel like it right now. Sorry."

She threw a pillow at me and would have knocked over my glass if I hadn't snatched it.

"Oops," she said. "Good save. Should we say something about preferring a man who uses mint mouthwash and breath mints?"

"You should. Yes. I'm going to say I have allergies, so he must be a consumer of all natural everything."

Toni filled her glass. "There's a question about political affiliation."

"Oh! I'm going to put that I'm a card-carrying member of the Surprise Party."

"Ha! Well, I would join you, but I'm a member of the Boston Tea Party. I've completely given up on the Vegetarian Party. I'm trying to increase my carbon footprint."

My side was hurting from laughing. "That's a good one. What should we put for our hobbies and interests?"

Toni thought for a second. "Extreme ironing."

I snorted my wine. "What about duck herding? I think that's legit. Oh! And I just read a crazy article about an incarcerated guy who made it into the Guinness Book of World Records for filing lawsuits." I changed my voice and posture as if I was on a first date. "Truly, suing people has been a profitable pastime for me. You should try it. You name it, I'll sue them."

Things devolved from that point.

"We have to stop," I cried when we finished the last question. "My throat hurts from laughing."

Toni gasped. "I can't breathe."

I tossed my package on the footstool. It was time for *I Love Lucy*, as if a comedy show would cure our laughter pains.

"We're not putting our names on these things, are we?" Toni finally said.

I shook my head. "No. We'll have to get new forms in the morning. At any rate, I'm not sure how serious Nell is about finding our soul mates since we weren't exactly on the hunt for life partners."

As I set up the DVD player, I briefly wondered why I was more eager to catch a killer, if there was one skulking around the resort, than I was to find love.

Chapter Six

THE NEXT MORNING, I woke with a gasp. I'd been dreaming about the murder again. This time, I clearly saw hands wearing gray gloves with wide slashes of orange holding a woman, likely Alicia, under the water.

My heart was pounding. I sat up and breathed slowly, in and out, calming myself in the dimly lit room. I checked my watch. Six-fifteen. The sun had risen. Things were always easier to deal with in the light of day.

It was rare for me to have the same dream more than once, if I ever had. Why was this dream different? The answer escaped me. My best guess was whoever murdered Alicia wore gray gloves with orange stripes. For unknown reasons, I'd tapped into that moment. Since I'd never dreamed about a murder before, I could only guess this one related to Alicia. The rowboat in my dream and the one in Nell's photo matched. I had to take a leap of faith and dig deeper. There could be a murderer on the loose, close to Nell.

By the time I showered, dressed in a blouse and skirt, and spent more than my usual five minutes on hair and makeup, I was feeling like my normal self.

Last night, Toni and I had been too tipsy and silly to concentrate. I needed a night like that every once in a while. We'd agreed to hit the dining room when it opened this morning, so we had time to talk strategy.

One of my favorite aromas greeted us as we walked into the dining room—coffee. By the look of the breakfast buffet, Great Bear Resort was pulling out all the stops, but I was determined to keep to my meal plan. I didn't want to think of it as a diet because that brought up all sorts of bad feelings about deprivation and hunger. As long as I kept to my calorie allotment, I'd be fine, so instead of over-doing it at the buffet, we ordered à la carte from a table with a sweeping view of the dining room, from where we hoped to spy on Lennox Huff in action.

I was an energetic person, but today I was especially pumped. Was it the adrenaline from the dream? Another mystery to solve. Pieces to fit together. Righting a wrong. Bringing a murderer to justice. The prospects were fuel to me.

Finishing up breakfast, we quietly discussed Alicia's case. How were we going to determine if Lennox had a credible motive to have killed her?

Toni wiped her mouth with a napkin. "Let's say Nell is right. Lennox killed Alicia because their breakup enraged him, and he just snapped. He could be a sociopath."

"Okay, so for the sake of argument, he snapped," I said. "If anyone could anger a person to a dangerous extent, it was Alicia. Maybe she was too arrogant or detached to have read warning signs if they were there. She was probably a narcissist. When we were kids, she liked to shame people. It seemed to amuse her to make someone cry. She picked on me for having frizzy hair, which could be why, to this day, I can't walk by a frizz-taming product without buying it."

"She sounds like a real gem," Toni said, patting her blonde curls. "Do you think she was like that as an adult? If so, there may be more suspects. What did Nell say about her?"

"Honestly, I got the impression Nell admired Alicia. People do change. But then again, Nell is so sweet, she doesn't say anything negative about anyone. It would be just like her to only see Alicia's positive qualities. In all fairness, it sounded like she had a few."

Toni smiled. "Generous of you to say."

"I know. Thank you for noticing." As I took a sip of coffee, I realized something. "My exposure to Alicia is mainly from school days. That's colored my opinion of her. I'm going to have to rise above my childhood feelings and see her with more objectivity."

"Sounds sensible. So, why don't we each have a conversation with Lennox, then compare notes? Maybe we should ask him the same questions and see if his answers are consistent?"

I nabbed the last piece of tomato from my plate. "Good idea. And let's come up with questions that might give us insight into his propensity for vindictiveness or unchecked rage."

Toni stared at me over her coffee cup. "Our conversations sure have changed since we became the Murder Gals."

Our brainstorming session ended when a woman with a microphone asked for everyone's attention. Since I'd had my head down for the last thirty minutes composing questions for Lennox, it surprised me to see the dining room filled. There must have been sixty people.

"Welcome, everyone, to Heart to Heart's Love Extravaganza!" The petite, curly-haired woman paused to allow for whistles and clapping, instigated by her enthusiastic welcome. She looked to be thirty-something and spunky. "Let me start by introducing myself. I'm Melody Pennycook, the event planner for this occasion. I'll be here for the next ten days to be sure things run smoothly. If you have questions about the event, I'm your girl." She paused to look over the crowd. "What a great-looking group of singles! Are you ready to find the love of your life?" This garnered another round of hoots and applause.

Or if that fails, you can join our find-the-killer team.

"Everyone at Heart to Heart has worked hard to bring you lovely people together based on your interviews and the profiling questions you answered."

Profile questions. Toni and I looked at each other. I bit back a laugh and made a mental note to grab another set and take it more seriously.

Melody pointed at a table of four women. "Your soul mates are here right now in this room just waiting to meet you. It's our job to help you connect, but I also want to be honest. There's a chance this won't work for you.

Over the next week, you'll see the number of people here dwindling—there won't be as many filling these chairs. Your matchmakers will talk to each of you to see how it's going. At the end of the week, they'll start whittling down the group by eliminating those who aren't gravitating toward anyone."

The volume in the room went up. Melody paused and then continued when things quieted. "You all know about the prize at the end of these ten days. We'll fly the couples with the deepest connections to Mexico and if love is true, we're going to have us some weddings!"

"I still find that hard to believe," I said to Toni.

"I'm with you." Toni hesitated, her gaze on someone across the room. "Quinn! I think that's him—Lennox." She whipped her head back to face me. "Don't stare at him. I think he saw me looking."

"Okay. Where is he?" I asked, without turning my head. Since he'd taken up Alicia on her offer to enter the matchmaking event, maybe he really had gotten over her like he said.

"About three tables away, close to the window. Green sweater, and he's facing us. There's a white-haired guy at his table. You can look now. He's got his eyes on Melody."

I turned, trying for casual, just a slow scan of the dining room. Green sweater. There. I paused and narrowed my focus, recalling the photo Nell had sent to me. "That's him," I verified. He'd had a haircut, shorter on the sides, but still salt and pepper. His complexion was naturally ruddy, I guessed. In the photo, I'd thought he had a sunburn.

The room broke into laughter. I'd missed whatever Melody had said, so I gave her my attention.

"So, now that you've had your caffeine, we're going to get started with a mixer. I suggest you keep the conversations short and try to talk to as many people as you can. You'll have all morning to get to know each other. Then, I'll ask you to submit the names of three people you'd like to spend more time with. We're hoping for matches, but if that's not the case, don't despair. There'll be more time to get to know people. That's your only job while you're here. So, everyone, please make your way into the lounge at the end of the hall. Go and mingle!"

"Do we have to?" Toni asked, raising her voice as chairs scraped across the floor and the volume in the room increased.

I sympathized with Toni, who was more introverted than I was. My need for social connections was one reason I opened a café. Toni was happiest on her own in the kitchen, although I never had to ask her for help up front with customers when things got busy. "Just try to have fun," I said. "At least we're all about the same age. This might have been a challenge if people were in their twenties."

Toni snorted. "Then we'd have to play house-mothers."

"Not me. I like my empty nest. Thank you very much." I tossed my napkin on the table and pushed back my chair.

"You head for Lennox first," I suggested. "I'll let some time pass before I talk to him, so hopefully he won't think our questions are too similar." We were going to throw in a few random questions, too. And I imagined the natural conversation would take us in different directions.

"I'm going to hit the bathroom first," Toni said. "Good luck!"

We'd been given name tags, notebooks, and pens to keep track of potential mates, but I wasn't planning to write about anything other than my suspicions. I pinned on my tag, stuffed the notebook into my purse for now, and headed over to the lounge.

Sunlight streamed in from windows unleashing a view of a massive deck and the lake beyond. A fieldstone fireplace, a white cedar bar, and potted shrubs made the lounge an extension of the outdoors. People perched on stools, leaned into couches. The room was humming.

I looked for Lennox and saw him talking to a bushy-haired woman. I recognized her from the outdoor campfires we'd seen last night.

Someone sidled up beside me. "Hi there. I'm Clark. Are you as uncomfortable getting a conversation going with strangers as I am?"

I laughed. "Well, that line works. And no, not really, but that's only because I own a café and have become fluent in small talk."

He smiled, crinkling his eyes. They were striking eyes—cobalt blue. He was a good-looking man. Wavy cinnamon-colored hair and a fit physique. "Fantastic. We already have something in common—I love coffee. What made you want to own your own business?"

"I'd been a stay-at-home mom for years and wanted to get back into the workforce, but things in the business world had changed so much my public relations degree was no longer relevant. I liked the idea of owning a business, loved to entertain, and I'd gotten pretty good at concocting specialty drinks and figured an artisan coffee shop was a good fit for me. It helps that I love coffee, too. So far, it's going really well."

"That's impressive...Quinn." When he looked down at my name tag, I realized I'd not introduced myself. "Since a good deal of coffee shops fail in their first year."

I knew that because my ex had drilled it into my head pretty much every day. "What do you do for a living?"

"Oh, boring stuff. I'm a corporate lawyer. Not nearly as interesting as owning a café."

I figured he was right about that. "Well then, what do you like to do for fun?"

"I've got a decent woodworking shop in my garage and exercising is important to me. I run, bike, ski, play tennis, and I've been hunting jackalopes with my brother. What about you?"

Since I didn't run, play tennis or ski and no longer owned a bicycle, I didn't want to discuss my exercise regime, which wholly consisted of walking and lifting ten-pound weights in my bedroom. "Jackalopes? I've never heard of them."

His eyes were full of life when he smiled. "They're said to be fascinating creatures and move at lightning speeds—a cross between a pygmy-deer and a rabbit."

I tried to picture that cross. "Really? And where do you hunt these creatures?"

"New Mexico, Colorado, and Wyoming where they're most commonly sighted. I try to catch them on film."

He seemed like a nice guy, and I was glad he hunted jackalopes to film not to kill. I was going to ask if he had photos when I saw Nell talking to Melody across the room. Behind them, I thought I saw a clown—a man with a painted face and a bulbous red nose—but when I blinked, he shimmered, and disappeared. Gone. Like a ghost. I scanned the room.

"Quinn?" Clark was looking at me, waiting for a response to something he'd asked.

No ghost. "I'm sorry. I got distracted. Can you say that again?"

"I was asking if you like to travel."

Why was the ghost a clown? "Travel? Well, other than a few holidays in the tropics, I'm not well-traveled, but I'd like to change that."

"I suppose owning your own business gives you flexibility to travel."

"Right. Yes, well, hopefully one day when I can let go, I guess."

Had I seen a ghost? Nell and Melody were looking at something on an iPad and wouldn't have noticed the clown behind them. No one else reacted to it. He couldn't have gotten out of the room that quickly. Must have been a ghost. I glanced behind me. Nothing. Maybe it was gone for good.

"Well, I don't want to monopolize your time," Clark said. "It was nice meeting you. Good luck." He made a beeline for a woman standing alone.

Guessing I'd blown that potential love connection, I headed to the bathroom to get my thoughts in order. After using the facilities, I stood in front of the mirror thinking about the clown, but Clark's twinkling eyes kept drifting into my thoughts. It couldn't have been more than five minutes, but he'd actually made an impression on me—who'd have guessed that could happen so fast? He'd been easy to talk to and easy on the eyes. As for the clown... A ghost? Or a trick of the eye. The artwork in the lounge was full of bright colors.

I checked my watch. Only twenty minutes had passed. It wasn't time for me to grill Lennox yet, so I'd better get out there and talk to more men. If I brought up Alicia, maybe I could learn something. I left the bathroom and headed down the hall into the lounge, where I met Nell.

She winked at me. "How's it going?"

"No love connections yet," I said, then lowered my voice as I saw Toni talking to Lennox. She was laughing. "We're taking this opportunity to get to know Lennox."

She nodded. "Good. And thank you for getting your profiles done so quickly."

"Profiles?" As far as I knew, the ones Toni and I had fabricated were still in our room.

"Courtney just found them on the desk in our office space. We haven't had a chance to go through them yet, but my staff is on it. And I'll do my best to be sure you and Toni get everything you asked for."

What? How did they get handed in? We sure didn't do it. Could the cleaning staff have thought they were doing us a favor?

I gulped, recalling how ridiculous our answers had gotten by the end of the form. When asked to give an example of a relationship deal breaker, Toni had written cheese-eaters and I'd said men in cartels. Oh gosh. I couldn't see myself admitting to Nell that we'd made a farce out of her forms. Best scenario was that Nell was mistaken.

A woman's scream cut through the room, freezing me in place.

"What's happened?" Nell cried, spinning around.

One of the staff had just entered the lounge through the kitchen. Still screaming, she slapped her her hair and her shoulders. Little black things dotted the surrounding floor. "Spiders! They're on me! Get them off!"

Nell ran to the woman. I was close behind. The sight of the eight-legged arachnids on her white blouse made me shudder. A man had already gotten to her and was holding one spider in the palm of his hand.

"We'll get them off," Nell said, looking startled as she brushed one from the woman's back.

"Hold on," the man said. Anthony, according to his name tag. "They're not real. They're plastic."

The victim stopped screaming. "What? Plastic?" She plucked one from her arm and held it with her fingertips. "What the...?"

Nell flushed. "I'm at a loss. And I'm so sorry. I don't know what's happened here."

The recovering woman pointed to the doorway she'd come through. "They fell on me as I came through the door."

I spied a piece of white netting on the floor. Almost invisible since the tile was a creamy color. I picked it up and dangled it in front of me. "They must have been in this."

"Ew!" someone cried behind me. "Are those spiders?"

"They're not real," Nell said to the milling crowd. "Someone's idea of a bad joke. I'm sorry for the interruption and for your fright," she said to the staff member while checking her hair. "Why don't you go to the ladies' room and make sure they're all gone?"

Another server appeared. "I'll sweep this up," he said.

Toni joined us and took in the spiders. "If it was close to Halloween, I'd understand," she said.

"I guess we have a prankster among us." I looked through the crowd. That's when I saw the clown again. As we made eye contact, he locked onto my gaze and stared at me with his painted smile. Then he shimmered again. He wasn't fully opaque. I'd been right. Ghost. I shook my head in dismay, wondering what kind of trouble this one would bring.

Chapter Seven

I WASN'T GOING TO let that ghost-clown think he could start haunting me just because we'd made eye contact, so I flicked my head, indicating he should follow me outside where we could talk. I needed to get the upper hand right away. Some ghosts were shysters, and even if they seemed decent, they always had their own agendas and were passionate about achieving them. Everyone I'd met was either a murder victim or related somehow to the case I was trying to solve. I couldn't imagine how a clown was related to Alicia's death, but I wanted to talk to him nonetheless. In my limited experience, I'd learned ghosts loved to talk to living people, so I figured he'd follow me.

"I'll be right back," I said to Toni.

As I grabbed my coat, I wondered how her conversation with Lennox had gone. Fairly well, I assumed by her cheerful, relaxed demeanor.

Once I was outside, I headed toward our cabin, thinking I could also check to see if someone took the profiles Toni and I filled in last night from the room. I couldn't say I was feeling as relaxed as Toni appeared to be, especially since that spider incident had given me the willies, and the ghost hadn't helped.

Sure enough, the clown fell into step beside me.

"Glory me!" he said. "What a day this is. You not only see ghosts, but if I were to judge you by the energy you're giving off, there's something special about you. Are you a witch?"

My eyebrows hit my hairline. I threw him an are-you-insane look. If this ghost was going to try to trick me into welcoming witches into my life, not that I believed in such things, we would not have a pleasant conversation. My Aunt Elsie said if you didn't acknowledge the supernatural, they didn't gain a foothold in your life. I didn't know if that was true, but I figured a good dose of denial couldn't hurt me in this case. "Definitely not. There are no such things as witches." I was walking fast and felt my rapid heartbeat, probably from clown-induced stress.

"You believe in ghosts, but not witches? What about angels, demons, vampires, elves, fairies?"

I laughed. "You're putting me on, right? My life is weird enough as it is." According to Aunt Elsie, faeries had blessed me at birth, a blessing that would deliver a bounty in midlife, and hopefully hadn't meant my burgeoning waistline. No, I'd receive a gift I was supposed to develop. I was taking it to mean my ability to see dead people as well as my relationship with Brielle and our working together to solve the mysteries that came our way.

The ghost and I reached the turn in the road that led to my cabin. Since there was no one around, it seemed safe to talk. Now that I had a good look at him, he didn't seem as frightful as my first glance. I took in what appeared to be a friendly face, although it could have been the face paint. Hazel eyes were set in white half circles with high black commas for eyebrows. Rosy cheeks flanked a typical clown nose. A miniature red hat sat atop his puffy blue hair.

"Let's talk about you," I said. "Who are you, and why are you here?"

"Aren't you a direct crumpet," he said. "I like that. I'm Moe Sutherland, previously known as Jolly Moe, clown for hire." He tipped his hat. "You remind me of her. Maybe you're as misunderstood. Hmm?"

Misunderstood? "Who are you talking about?"

"Well, Alicia Smallwood, of course. Isn't that why you're here? You and your friend Toni."

It disturbed me to think he'd been spying on us. Although that seemed rather hypocritical since Toni and I were making spying an art form. "How'd you know that?"

He laughed. "I have my ways. Oh, don't start fretting, Quinn. I've been hanging around Nell and the gang ever since Alicia passed. I know Nell intended to bring you here to help figure out what happened to Alicia."

This was promising. It could be helpful to have a ghost poking around. "What do *you* think happened to Alicia?"

He gave a dismissive gesture. "It hardly matters to me. Everyone has their time to go—it's fate, pumpkin. I don't get caught up in the details of the dearly departed. I'm here for the living."

I stopped to dig through my purse to find the key card. "How can you be here for the living?"

"Pardon? Can I help you with something?"

"What?" I looked up to see a man coming down the steps of the cabin next to ours. I'd had my head down and hadn't noticed him. It took me a second to realize he was speaking to me.

"Um, no. I'm good, thanks."

He stopped beside me. His gaze went to my ears as if looking for the earbuds I usually wore, so people would think I was on the phone and not talking to myself.

"You said something about being here for the living," the olive-skinned man said. Built like a brick house, he blocked out the sun.

"I don't think so. I mean, maybe." I forced a laugh. "Sometimes I talk things out when I've got a problem to solve. Drives people crazy when I do that. Don't mind me."

The guy gave me a skeptical look.

Moe started to laugh. I forced myself not to look at him. He reached over and tickled the top of the man's ear. The guy brushed him away.

This was one juvenile clown.

"Have a good day!" I said cheerfully and started walking.

"Good luck with your problem-solving."

"Yep. Thanks." I hurried up the steps into the cabin, then closed the door. A few seconds later, Moe materialized in the room, his mouth perpetually happy and a smile in his eyes.

I dropped my purse on the floor. "Okay. You've got my attention, but not for long. What do you want?"

He cocked his head and put his hands out, palms up. "Isn't it obvious? To make people laugh, silly. I wouldn't be much of a clown otherwise. My job is to generate the three G's—giggles, guffaws, and glee." He squeezed the flower in his lapel, and I scooted out of the way, expecting a stream of water to hit me in the face.

This produced a belly laugh from the clown. "If only my pansy would work, but alas, I can't get the water to stay in the reservoir. Just keeps falling through."

I let out my breath, pressing my lips together to prevent a smile. I didn't want to encourage him. "So, you entertain other spirits?"

"Sometimes. But when someone like Alicia dies, I come to ease the suffering of her loved ones with a few pranks. Provides a distraction from their grief, you know."

None of these people were grieving, but I didn't point that out. "People like Alicia?"

"I mean, friends like Alicia. I considered her a friend after we met a couple of years ago when we were roommates in the hospital. We'd both been in car accidents—not the same accident—she was admitted after me. She'd suffered multiple leg fractures. I'd smashed my cheek bone and broken my jaw." He pushed his lips out in an exaggerated frown which didn't quite work. "When she learned I was a clown, she made it her mission to keep us both entertained by reading aloud some of the funniest books ever written."

"Really? She did that?"

"She sure did." He paused and frowned, I think. It was hard to tell with his permanent smile. "I know what it's like to grieve. I died of a broken heart when my wife passed. Couldn't live without my best friend."

I felt for Moe. When I was a teenager, a friend's mom suffered a fatal heart attack two days after her husband died. People said she died of a broken heart. "I'm sorry you suffered a loss like that."

He gave a dismissive gesture. "It's not a loss any longer. But it's the reason I'm here providing comedic relief for Alicia's staff, so the fruits of her labors flourish as she'd dreamed they would."

"Wait a minute. Were you the one who hung a net of plastic spiders over the doorway?"

He laughed and kept on laughing until he couldn't catch his breath. The man was so naturally jovial, just watching him laugh had me erupting despite my intentions to keep a straight face.

"Moe, stop," I finally said. "Those spiders weren't funny. They freaked out the woman who got doused. She'll probably have nightmares."

"Oh, I don't think so, pumpkin. She's going to be preoccupied with the man who came to her rescue—that's what I think. Alicia's not the only matchmaker in the fold."

I'd met a spread-the-cheer, matchmaking, ghost-clown. Who would believe my life? "I know you said you're not interested in Alicia's death, but Nell thinks someone murdered Alicia. Nell is my friend, so I promised to do a little digging to see if she's right. Can't you find

Alicia and talk to her? See if she can provide any insight into her death."

He started laughing again. "Toss aside my values as if they were trash? Do the opposite of everything I'm trying to accomplish? I will not remind Alicia of her tragic death."

I gave him a look. He was being rather dramatic. "I'm not asking you to throw anything in the trash. Won't it be impossible for her to rest in peace if she believes her killer got away scot-free?"

He tapped his chin with his finger. "I don't know. I'll tell you what. I'll think about it, if you'll go back to the mixer and take it seriously—at least try to find true love."

"I said I'm here to help Nell. How do you know I haven't already found true love?"

"Oh, I know, crumpet. I've been poking around. I know you and your friend are single."

"Okay, fine. I'll have a few serious conversations while you find Alicia in the afterlife."

He reached down and picked up my purse, offering it to me. I didn't take it. "I'm going to use the bathroom, which is your cue to leave, please."

"Then I will bid you a good day." He blew me a kiss and bowed low, then lower, then lower, until his nose brushed against the top of my black pumps. I guess I'd have to be a ghost before I was nearly as flexible. His back shook with giggles.

"Oh, brother. Goodbye, Moe." I side-stepped, scooted into the bathroom, and closed the door. I was about to turn the lock, but what good would that do? Pressing my ear against the door, I listened for signs he was still hanging around. After hearing nothing, I decided if I was going to worry about him invading my privacy, I was going to get rather uncomfortable.

A couple minutes later, I left the bathroom, relieved to see our room was clown free. I paused for a moment, trying to remember what else I meant to do. Ah...the profile questions. I was pretty sure they'd been on the ottoman, but housekeeping had already been in, and there was no sign of the forms. I really didn't want Nell or her team getting their hands on those things. I had to get those papers back.

Geez, it was a good thing I wasn't looking for true love. I had no time. And I still had to grill Lennox.

I grabbed my purse and left the room, hurrying back to the main lodge.

Back in the lounge, I scanned the crowd for Toni. The beautifully dressed people, partnered up, appeared to be having a good time. I saw Toni sitting on a sofa talking to Lennox—again. They'd gravitated back to each other. I knew why she'd singled him out, but I found it interesting he wasn't trying to meet more women.

I was standing alone near the fireplace when someone came up beside me. "What a nice-looking group of people."

"I was just thinking the same thing," I said, recognizing Brielle's voice. "I'm glad I—" Ack! My brain had hiccupped over the fact she was invisible to others, like the ghost I'd been caught talking to earlier. And wouldn't it just figure the guy, built like a brick house, who'd seen me talking to Moe was now staring at me?

Great, just great.

Chapter Eight

AFTER FLASHING THE BRICK house guy a confidant smile, I headed out of the lounge toward the reception area. What was Brielle doing here so early in the day? I did a quick calculation and realized she must be having an afternoon nap to make up for all the sleep she lost.

She caught up with me. "This looks like fun, Quinn? Where are you?"

This time, I'd be smarter and not answer her until I rifled through my purse, found my earbuds, and stuffed them in. "Follow me." Down the hall in the opposite direction of the dining room, I found a bench where I could sit and pretend to be on a phone call.

"It's a matchmaking event," I said and took a few minutes to fill her in on my dream, hypnosis, Alicia's death, Nell's concern, and the event. Then I took a deep breath.

"I remember Alicia Smallwood. Not to speak ill of the dead, but she wasn't the nicest kid," Brielle said.

"I know. I feel the same way, but she didn't deserve to die like that, of course."

"No, of course not. You're sure your dream was Alicia's murder?" She tilted her head, studying me. "And you look great, by the way. You should dress up more often."

"Thank you, and I would, but a café's not the best place for good clothes. And yes, I'm ninety-nine percent sure my dream was Alicia's murder."

"Sounds like it," she said. "I suppose it would be a strange coincidence otherwise."

"Yes. As long as I didn't sleep-murder Alicia because she snubbed me at the grocery store."

Brielle gave me a look. "I hope you're kidding. You're not a murderer, awake or asleep. I doubt very much one of us could cause a death in an alternate universe. And by the sounds of it, you weren't in an alternate universe, anyway. It feels quite different from a dream. I'm much more cognizant and aware of myself when I'm in your life. The events that happen here aren't haphazard like they are in a dream. I think what you experienced was a psychic episode, Quinn. Like the time we saw Mrs. Cavan's death."

I'd been eleven or twelve years old when that happened. Mrs. Cavan had driven her car off a bridge, and the vision of her blue Volkswagen hitting the water had popped into my head before the accident happened.

"When did you have the dream about the drowning?"

I knew exactly when. "Last Saturday."

"And when did Alicia die?"

"Sunday morning." I'd completely missed that fact. Or maybe I'd not considered it on purpose because it was horrifying to have predicted a murder, especially when

I'd not seen the victim or the killer. How was something like that of any use?

"See what I mean, Quinn? You had a psychic dream that predicted Alicia's death."

I felt like throwing up. "I don't want to have death dreams! How do I make them stop?"

Sympathy washed over her face. "I don't know. But maybe we can figure it out. Oh, Quinn, I'm sorry this has happened to you."

I tried to buck up, considering Brielle had her own supernatural mishaps to deal with. "We sure are special, aren't we?"

"I have to believe our *specialness* is for a good reason, or I'll go nuts. I'm curious about something, though. Why didn't you talk to Aunt Elsie about your dream?"

It was a valid question because our aunt had been a dream therapist. "Because I was terrified I'd been involved in a homicide, and I didn't want to worry her."

"Oh, Quinn. I wish you had a man like Julien to remind you how futile worrying is. He'd say don't spend your energy thinking of things you don't want to happen. Seriously. What's the point?"

Julien sure was perfection. I knew worrying was a waste of time, but sometimes it was easier said than done. Yet, talking it over with Brielle, the only person who truly understood my weird life, had made me feel better. "Julien-the-extraordinary is right."

She laughed. "I can't help singing his praises. He seems to consume my sleeping thoughts, too, apparently."

Yes, he certainly was all consuming. *Do I want to be so preoccupied by a man?* "I'm sorry, Brielle, but I've got to get back to this event."

"Tell me what I can do to help. Remember, I'm supposed to be a member of the Murder Gals team."

"I really don't like that name, but I do need your help." I told her about the profiles Toni and I had filled in last night. "Nell has office space here. Do you think you could snoop around and destroy those forms? They should be on a desk."

"Absolutely." She stood. "I better do it quickly. And, Quinn, I want you to find as good a man as Julien, so do take this experience seriously, although I don't think you need to look further than the park ranger. I'm rooting for him."

Again, with Alec. "I'll do my best."

I took a moment to compose myself, then headed back to the lounge. Toni was still talking to Lennox. Since she'd obviously lost track of time, I tried to make eye contact, but she was doing a good job making him think he'd engrossed her in whatever he was saying. Okay. Well, I'd promised to give this event a try, so I sidled over to the window when a man, sans woman, looked my way.

Over the next hour, I had wonderful conversations with Gregory, a master brewer, Keith, a sugar beet farmer, and Mac, a security guard. All of them were bright, interesting, and easy to talk to. I had to commend Heart to Heart. They really had done their due diligence when selecting singles for this event, which made me even more eager to get those idiotic profiles into the trash. There'd been no sign of Brielle, so I didn't know if she'd accomplished this.

I was talking to Mac when I saw the dark-haired guy, who'd caught me talking to myself—twice—look my way and say something to his companion. She turned, stared at me, and laughed. *At me? Did he tell her I was cuckoo?* I caught her eye, then his, and smiled widely like the dingbat they must have thought I was. They both turned away.

"You have an admirer?" Mac asked, following my gaze. "Or two?"

"Oh, I don't think so. They've probably mistaken me for someone else."

"Everyone, can I get your attention, please?" Melody called from the front of the room. "I hope you all had a good time getting to know each other. The mixer has concluded, and now I need you to grab a slip of paper from the bar and write the names of three people you'd like to spend more time with. Our matchmakers will do their magic, and tomorrow morning I'll announce who you'll have your first one-on-one date with. Don't worry if you haven't made a connection yet. We'll take care of it. Everyone will have a one-on-one with someone. For now, feel free to keep the conversations going or enjoy the resort."

"I'd love to spend more time with you and hear more about your new grandson," Mac said. "There's nothing I like better than being a grandpa."

I appreciated that since I didn't feel I'd been fully present during our conversation. I wasn't sure if he meant right now or if he was talking about a one-on-one date. "That would be nice. I'd like that, too. Unfortunately, I've got to check in at my café."

"Sure. Sure, that's fine. Don't work too hard, though." He shook my hand. His grip was intense, bordering on painful. *Shoot. He was nervous. Did he think I was rejecting him?* "See ya later."

"I'd really like that!" I said with too much alacrity as he walked away. I was not good at this dating business.

I looked for Toni and saw her saying goodbye to a good-looking, tall guy who towered over her barely five-foot frame.

She was smiling as she joined me. "I'm surprised to admit this, but that was more fun that I imagined."

I couldn't say the same, but not because of poor company. Things had gotten a little harried for me, so I hardly remembered what I'd talked about with the men. "Fun, huh? That's great. So...who were you having this fun with? The guy you were just talking to? He's pretty good looking."

She shook her head, made a clicking sound with her tongue. "No, not him."

I'd not been paying close attention, but the only man I'd seen her talking to was Lennox, our murder suspect. "Well, who then? Hurry and point him out before he leaves."

"Oh, well, it's not that important. What I meant was, it just wasn't as difficult to talk to men as I'd expected. I could do more of it...if need be."

"I'm glad you're enjoying yourself. There's no reason you can't mix business and pleasure."

"What about you?" she asked. "Do you have a man or two or three in mind for a one-on-one?"

I could put Mac's name down. Maybe Clark. "Yes, although I'd rather focus on...you know." I didn't want to mention the word murder out loud. "You should put Lennox's name on your list in case we have more questions. I didn't get a chance to talk to him, but I'm eager to hear about your conversation."

"It was enlightening, and I will put his name on my list. I'll go do that right now and meet you in the room."

I was glad to see her getting into this. "Okay. We have a few things to talk about, then I'm going to go into Break Thyme for a couple of hours."

"See you in a few."

Since I didn't know if Brielle had destroyed our profiles, I wanted to talk to Nell first. I decided to be up front and say we'd made mistakes on the forms and wanted to redo them.

At reception, I asked where to find the Heart to Heart office and learned it was a room in the business center. As I approached the door, Melody was leaving.

"Hi, Melody. I'm Quinn, a friend of Nell's. Do you know where I can find her?"

She shook my hand. "It's nice to meet you, Quinn. No. I've not seen Nell since the spider incident. She's probably being extra vigilant, worried about what might happen next."

Moe's practical joke. "Oh, well, it seemed like a harmless prank. She's not really worried about it, is she?"

Melody flicked her chin. Her gaze fixed on something behind me. "You can ask her yourself. Here she comes."

I turned to see Nell looking strained. The crinkles around her eyes were more pronounced. Running an event like this was enough to cause tension under the best of circumstances. She was worried about Alicia's murder and pranks that might derail things.

"We've got a problem," Nell said, looking at Melody and then at me. "Can we step inside the office, please? Quinn, you're a great sounding board, so I'd love your thoughts if you have a minute."

Once we were inside and Nell closed the door, she said, "I'm concerned that Becca is at it again."

Melody sighed. "I was worried about that."

"Who's Becca?" I asked.

"Becca runs Cupid Connection, the other matchmakers in the competition for the reality series," Nell said.

"What are you concerned about?" I asked.

"Those fake spiders, for one. I think Becca has planted a troublemaker as one of our participants."

Oh, dear. I couldn't tell her the spiders were the work of Moe, the ghost-clown. "That seems rather underhanded for a professional, no?"

"You don't know Becca," Melody said. "I've worked with her. She's not above doing something like that at all. She's devious and scheming."

"Sadly, that's true," Nell said. "At one of our events last month, all of our gluten-free meals went missing. And then, all the cutlery disappeared from the tables. My notes went missing from the podium. It made us look unprofessional."

"How do you know these things were Becca and not problems with the venue?" I asked.

"Because I recognized one of her staff," Melody said. "When she realized she'd been spotted, she ran to her car and left the event. Why would she do that if she wasn't up to no good?"

"I don't know," I admitted. "That is strange, I suppose."

"There's a history of animosity between Heart to Heart and Cupid Connection," Nell said. "Alicia and Becca didn't like each other."

Melody snorted. "That's an understatement."

My interest perked up. Why hadn't Nell mentioned this before? It sounded like Becca was a potential suspect. "Why do you say that, Melody?" I asked.

"Because I saw Becca and Alicia get into an argument. It was nasty. I honestly thought one of them might hit the other."

"Pardon me?" Nell said. "When did you see this?"

"In Minneapolis, in the parking lot of the Hyatt when we were there for the preliminary meetings."

"What were they arguing about?" I asked.

Melody jabbed her hand through her short, dark curls. "I didn't hear it all, but it sounded like Alicia was accusing Becca of maligning Heart to Heart on social media, something about sharing their clients' personal information for promotional purposes. But when I checked Cupid

Connection's social media sites, I couldn't find anything. Maybe it had been deleted after the damage was done."

Nell let out an exasperated breath. "I knew about that incident, but I didn't know Alicia and Becca nearly came to blows. I wish you'd told me, Melody." Nell looked at me. "It happened a few months ago, after Christmas. Alicia was certainly angry at the time. She talked about suing Cupid Connection for defamation, but the post *was* taken down, and Alicia let it go."

Hmm, if there were threats between Alicia and Becca, it was reason enough to add Becca to my list of suspects. If Becca stole meals from Heart to Heart's event, had Alicia retaliated with a stunt or two of her own?

Before I could ask, there was a knock on the door. Nell opened it to find one of the resort's servers. "Sorry to interrupt, but you should come and see this," she said.

Nell looked at me and grimaced. "Oh no. What is it?"

"It needs to be seen," the woman said.

The three of us followed the petite woman into the dining room to the coffee and tea station that also offered fruit and baked goods, in case anyone was hungry. A crowd had gathered, many people laughing. We needed to excuse our way through to get closer.

Every item on the table wore a pair of googly eyes. Everything. Eyes on the coffeemaker, tea bags, mugs, water glasses, muffin cups, granola bars, oranges and bananas. All different sizes and colors. All those eyes looking out at us made everything feel personified. I stifled a laugh.

Nell had a tight smile on her face.

"We hope you get a kick out of this," said Melody to the crowd. "It's our mission to keep everyone smiling!"

Good one, Melody. I looked around for signs of Moe, and sure enough, there he was in the room's corner, bent over in laughter. He rose, looked my way, and winked. I just rolled my eyes.

Nell looked like she wanted to strangle someone. Probably Becca. I couldn't think of anything to say as Nell stormed off, Melody on her tail.

In all the excitement, I'd forgotten to ask for our profile submissions to be returned. And now, Toni was waiting for me in the room, Nell was on a rampage, and I needed to get to Break Thyme. For now, I'd have to hope that Brielle had successfully intercepted our idiotic paperwork.

I headed back to the room, eager to hear what Toni thought of Lennox Huff. I just had one niggling concern. It was probably nothing, but I couldn't help feeling a little discomfort at the way Toni had been smiling at our potential murder suspect. I didn't think she was that good an actor.

Chapter Nine

BACK IN THE PRIVACY of our room, Toni and I were able to talk about her conversation with Lennox. I was eager to hear what she thought of him as our number one suspect.

She rubbed the back of her neck as if she was feeling tense. "If Lennox did kill Alicia, and he's *not* a psychopath but has a normal conscience, I figured he'd suffer some remorse and want to avoid a conversation about her."

That was reasonable. "So, you brought Alicia up?"

"Yes, like we discussed, I said I was friends with Nell and was sad to have learned of Alicia's death. Right away, Lennox admitted to knowing Alicia. He seemed sincere when he said her death was a tragedy and had upset him. He even admitted they'd dated last summer."

"Hmm. Maybe he's being savvy by keeping to as much of the truth as possible."

Toni shook her head. "I don't think so. My first impression of him was favorable. He's a really nice man."

"Okay, but people have said that about serial killers. They're charming for a reason."

"Oh, for goodness' sake, Quinn. I hardly think Lennox is a serial killer."

"I didn't mean he was," I said, but I was concerned about her sounding defensive.

She grabbed her purse from the counter. "I still have a bit of a headache after all that wine we drank last night."

Ah, she wasn't feeling well. "I'm sorry your head hurts, and I do trust your judgment, by the way."

She retrieved her vial of peppermint oil and rolled it over her forehead. "Thank you. You *can* trust me to be objective, especially since I just met the man. "

"I know. So, you asked him about his relationship with Alicia?"

"Yes, I did. He said he was the one who ended it with Alicia because she was becoming too controlling, and he's too old for that nonsense. He didn't seem to harbor any resentment toward her. From his perspective, the breakup was amiable."

"That's odd, because Nell suggested the opposite."

"Well, I don't know about that. I'm just giving you the facts as I see them."

"Right. Okay, so were you able to find out if he had an alibi for Sunday morning?"

She frowned. "No, I wasn't. I guess I got caught up in the conversation."

I waited for her to elaborate, but she said nothing further. After years of showing no interest in men, I didn't know what I'd do if she fell for a potential murder suspect. I stretched my neck to relieve some tension. I was jumping ahead, and that wasn't fair. Just because she said he was a nice guy didn't mean she was falling for him. No need to think that. She looked tired and probably hadn't slept well, so I didn't want to give her a hard time.

"I'm glad you had a good morning," I said, keeping things light. "It was rather fun to talk to a few men."

"I thought so, too, and that took me by surprise. The Heart to Heart people did a good job selecting candidates for this competition. I wanted to continue all the conversations I had. I liked every man I spoke with."

"Me, too, although I don't know that they'd say the same." I told Toni about the dark-haired guy who'd seen me talking to Moe and Brielle. "I think he's warning people away from me."

Toni scoffed. "Well, that's their loss, then. So, tell me more about the ghost."

I filled her in, then told her about the googly eyes and what Melody and Nell had said about Becca, the competition.

"It sounds like we've got another suspect," Toni said. "Unless you're clowning around?"

I gave her a look but was happy we'd cleared the air.

"So, clown-buster, what do you want to do next?" she asked.

"I told Poppy I'd come in this afternoon because she'll be working alone. As a matter of fact, I have to get going. But I think we should pay Becca a visit. I'll talk to Nell and get the details of where to find her."

"Do you want me to come with you to Break Thyme?"

"No. Why should both of us leave this paradise? We'll be fine, and if it's not busy, I'll give Poppy a well-deserved break."

"Well, if you insist, and in that case, I'm going to put on my bathing suit and go for a swim. The exercise may help my head."

After I'd arrived at Break Thyme and sent Poppy home, I was checking on the blackberries I'd strained for a cordial when Alec came in the door.

The sight of him sent a spark of excitement through me. No one else did that to me. He had a magnificent smile, one that had me smiling right back. It looked like he'd had a haircut, but not too short that he'd lost his sexy, tousled look.

"Hey, you," he said, coming up to the counter. "I've been missing your pretty face and lively companionship. How are you?"

You missed me? That's nice to hear. "I'm great. And even better now that you've dropped by." Maybe it was the romantic theme running through my life lately, but that sentiment seemed to have slipped out without my usual gatekeeping.

"Ah, I like that. Good to know." He slid up onto a stool. "How's Gabriel doing?"

Jordan had brought Gabriel in earlier for us to have a visit. I loved talking about him and did so for the next five minutes, showing Alec the most recent pictures.

"There's nothing like a baby, is there?" he said. "He's lucky to have you for his grandma."

"That's kind, Alec. So, what can I get you?"

"There's not a scone on the planet that can beat your strawberry almond. I hope I'm not too late in the day for one. Do you have any left?"

"I'll check in the kitchen. Be right back." I was humming as I opened the plastic container where we kept extra scones. It was Alec's lucky day—one left. I added a dollop of clotted cream and topped it with sliced strawberries.

I set the plate and fork in front of him and stood back, admiring the man and the dessert. I enjoyed the way Alec made me feel, maybe even more than dessert.

He licked his lips. "Wow. Look at that. Will you share it with me?"

"No, thank you. I'm determined to keep to my calorie count. But I will have a decaf with you if you'd like one."

"Sure, but I don't know why you think you need to count calories. You look fabulous to me."

I think I blushed, at least my body temperature rose a degree. It could have been a hot flash, but I didn't think so. There was something about this man, some unspoken chemistry, maybe a pheromone kind of thing that made me more aware of my skin.

"Keep those compliments coming, and there'll always be a scone here with your name on it," I replied and turned to pour us each a coffee.

"Deal. So, when are you moving back into the park?" he asked as I set a mug in front of him.

Probably as soon as I'd figured out who killed Alicia. It was hard to sleep with that dream hanging over my pillow every night. I'd not signed up to be a midlife crusader for justice, yet mysteries fell in my lap. I had to act.

My strongest regrets related to the things I didn't do. Opportunities I didn't pursue. Chances I didn't take. This was one reason opening my café had been vital to me. I didn't want to regret having never given it a try.

"Quinn? You look like you drifted away."

"Oh gosh, I'm sorry. I did drift. You had me thinking about the things I need to get done before moving back to Beach Meadows." In truth, I'd hardly thought about all the moving details.

"Okay, then. Tell me what I can do to help. Longfellow needs a spring check up. I can help you with that, if you like?"

Now a list of things flashed through my head—checking tire pressure and batteries, flushing and sanitizing the water system, spring cleaning the interior and exterior—to name a few. And a few things I'd yet to figure out. Having Alec help with all that would be a huge relief.

"Alec, I'd really appreciate your help, but only if you can spare the time. You must have a million things to do getting the park ready for the new season. And I'll be pretty busy for the next couple of weeks."

His gaze grew soft as he caught my eye. "Spending time with you will be a pleasure."

My body temperature went up another degree. He was being more flirty than usual today, and a big part of me liked it, but now a layer of perspiration was breaking out at my hairline. Oh dear. I hadn't had an internal heatwave like this in a few months.

"I like that idea, too. Um, excuse me for just a second." I pushed the scone closer to him, in the hope he'd be pleasantly occupied, while I swiped sweat from my face and down the middle of my back before I started to drip. Ugh, I thought my hot flashes were finished. *You're never completely finished, peanut*, came my mother's voice into my head.

In the kitchen, I grabbed a clean dish towel from the drawer and swabbed myself. Was there a more nefarious reason behind my hot flash? Was Alec's flirtatious behavior stressing me out? I liked him a lot, valued his friendship, but I also liked my single life and didn't want to change things—physical relationships changed things.

I retrieved the peppermint oil I used to cool down and dabbed a few drops onto the back of my neck. I'd feel its cooling effect soon and maybe then I'd be better able to relax.

Alec looked up when I joined him. "Another thing I've been thinking about lately is that I'd love to make dinner for you when you're free," he said. "I know how you like a star-lit sky, so I'll order one and arrange a few other touches." Heat flickered in his gaze.

Touches? It seemed as though he was testing the waters to see if I was ready to take our relationship to a romantic level. *Was I?* Why did this feel like a life-changing decision? It was only dinner. I could do dinner. "That sounds nice, Alec. I'd love that."

A purple bottle sat on the counter by his elbow. *Where did that come from?* It looked like a lotion of some sort. The bottle hadn't been there before I'd gone into the kitchen, so he must have put it there. I read the label. Wild Orchid Massage Oil. He really wanted to move our relationship out of the friend zone—and he wasn't being subtle about it either.

"A few other touches, huh?" I said, lifting my chin toward the oil. "That's a rather intimate suggestion."

"Hmm?"

"Are wild orchids a favorite of yours?"

He cocked his head, looking perplexed. "Wild orchids? Uh, well, who doesn't like orchids? Why do you ask?"

I raised my eyebrows. Now, he was playing coy after setting massage oil on my counter. Maybe he hadn't realized what scent the oil carried. "Because your massage oil is wild orchid."

He narrowed his gaze as if he still didn't know what I was talking about.

"Very funny." I said and reached for the oil. My hand went right through it as if it had no substance. *It's not real!*

I pulled back and froze.

Good grief! *What's going on?*

"Quinn? Are you okay?"

I whipped my head from the oil to Alec. My eyes wide. My brain trying to compute but coming up empty. I swallowed. Nodded.

"Yes. Mmhmm." Nodded again. "I'm okay." I stopped my incessant nodding. "I thought I...um..." How to finish that sentence? I should explain why I'd been talking about massage oil suddenly, but my brain was a complete blank.

"How's the scone?" I said weakly.

He was still staring at me, obviously concerned, probably not caring a fig about the scone.

"You're sure you're okay. Do you want to sit down?"

"Noooo. No. No." *Stop saying no. Sit. Sit. Grab a stool and sit.* What if I fell through an imaginary stool and broke my butt?

Alec's phone rang. The sound startled me. I flinched, but he didn't notice. He'd turned away to pull the phone from his back pocket, glance at it, and turn it off. "It was Allison. I'll call her back later." His daughter.

The wild orchid massage oil was gone.

I swallowed. Okay, this wasn't the first time I'd seen something that wasn't there. First, a bottle of broken walnut oil that may not have been visible to anyone else. Now, I was seeing massage oil. I couldn't begin to understand why oil mirages were popping into my vision. What could it possibly mean? *Stop trying to make sense of this and salvage the conversation.*

"How is Allison?" I asked, thankful he'd provided a subject change.

"Good, as far as I know. She's been on a holiday with her mother, so probably wants to see her old man and vent now that she's home. Her mother can be challenging."

I remembered him talking about his ex-wife's dependency on him, but that had been nearly a year ago when I'd only been single for fifteen months. I'd still been getting comfortable in my new independence, not that I hadn't been self-sufficient in my marriage, especially since we'd basically lived separate lives under the same roof. But I'd not been ready to take on a romantic relationship with anyone and the thought of his needy ex-wife in the mix had further distanced me. Yet, I always perked up when Alec dropped by. We'd become good friends, sharing stories of our previous lives and hopes for the future. He seemed proud of my café's successes. I'd not talked much about the mysteries Toni and I had solved because they'd involved the supernatural—something I wasn't ready to share with Alec. But if I were to get into a serious relationship with any man, I'd have to feel comfortable sharing every facet of my life with him and the thought of doing that worried me. My ex-husband hadn't believed me when I'd told him I'd spoken to the ghost of his mistress. After nearly three decades together, he'd been sure I was mistaken or maybe delusional. I'd hate for Alec to think of me that way.

"So, what's your schedule like this week?" he asked, forking the last chunk of scone into his mouth.

"I have a busy week, unfortunately. Can I call you when things settle down?"

The bells over the door jingled as Ivy came in. She wasn't scheduled to work, so it surprised me to see her. "What's up, Ivy?"

"I can't find my phone and hope I left it in the kitchen." She flew past us.

Alec shrugged. "Kids."

"I didn't see it in there," I called to Ivy. For such a wise young woman, she was often forgetful. This wasn't the first time she'd left something behind. Alec and I smiled at each other as the sounds of a search started in the kitchen—drawers opening and closing. Items sliding across the counter.

"Hold on. Before you tear the place apart, I'll call you," I offered.

"Don't bother," she yelled. "My phone's out of battery."

"Oh, dear."

"Think about where you were the last time you had it," Alec called into the kitchen as I searched both counters up front.

I found the phone under the toaster oven. "It's here, Ivy."

She appeared with a look of gratitude. "Thank you! Moms are always good at finding things."

"True," I said. "Lotsa practice."

"Poppy told me about your matchmaking thing," Ivy said. "How's it going? Any hot dates yet?"

Oh no. What would Alec think of that? My stomach turned over at him thinking I'd rather see other men instead of him.

His brow raised. "You're on a dating site?" he asked.

"No. Not really. I mean, my friend owns a matchmaking service, and I'm helping her figure out..." It sounded weird to me to say I was conducting a murder investigation, but if I was even considering dating Alec, I had to be honest with him. "Well, you see, what happened was her business partner drowned, and she thinks this woman's death—who's actually an old friend of mine—may not have been an accident. So Toni and I are doing a little digging."

"Ah, you're on another case!" Ivy said. "That's why people call them the Murder Gals," she informed Alec.

"Murder Gals?" he said with a slight smile. "I did not know your reputation was widespread, Quinn Delaney."

"I don't think it's that widespread."

"I look forward to hearing more about your matchmaking investigation," he said. "Just promise me one thing."

"What's that?"

"Don't do anything dangerous. And maybe this is selfish of me to say, but I hope you don't fall in love along the way."

A pang of discomfort rose in me at the mention of falling in love. If I was ready for that, surely, I'd be excited. But I was also happy he wasn't backing out of dinner after my random mention of wild orchid oil. No wonder I was uncomfortable. How could I date anyone when I couldn't trust my own eyes? What would happen if I told Alec the truth?

No. I can't do it. Not yet. I talk to ghosts. I have a twin from a parallel universe. I'm hallucinating bottles of oil. That was a lot of trust. It might be easier for him to believe I'd lost my marbles.

Still, I wanted a star-lit dinner with Alec, but I needed to take things slow. It couldn't hurt to keep a little mystery alive, so I looked him in the eye and just smiled.

Chapter Ten

Back at Great Bear Resort, I sat in our room, texting Toni. She'd had dinner with a group of people and was now having drinks in the lounge. I said I'd join her at eight-thirty, which gave me time to have a shower.

A part of me wanted to crawl into a hole and stay there until I knew for sure everything I saw in front of me was concrete. I ran my hand over the top of the dresser, touching a water glass, a brochure, a packet of sugar, relieved to find everything in a solid state.

Questions flitted through my head. Did I have to touch everything to know I wasn't surrounded by mirages? How else could I tell the difference between reality and illusion? The bottles of oil could be the tip of the iceberg. Maybe I'd walked past other hallucinations and not known it. Did these illusions have anything to do with the psychic dream? If they were related, I couldn't imagine how. Was there a chance solving Alicia's murder would bring an end to this crazy making? Or was I set on a delusional crash course?

In the bathroom, I stripped off my clothes, put my hair in a cap, and stood under the hot water, wishing I had a mentor to learn from. But other than Colleen, the owner of Mystic Garden in Bookend Bay, I didn't know anyone who could shed light on my weird life.

Maybe I'd feel better if I got dressed up. When you looked good, you felt good, or so they said. At any rate, I couldn't live my life fearing delusion.

After my shower, I changed into one of my favorite splurges—a vintage floral swing dress that hugged me in all the right places. With my hair up, less a few curls to frame my face, I thought I'd cleaned up pretty good. And indeed, as I admired myself in the mirror, I started to feel more in control.

I'd handled all the craziness so far. I wasn't going to let a couple hallucinations turn me into a cave dweller.

You got this.

I left the room and walked over to the lodge. As I entered the lounge and looked for Toni, I smiled at Keith, the beet farmer, who was talking to Gregory, the master brewer.

Toni was sitting with a small group by the window. Lennox looked pretty comfortable beside her on the couch, turned toward her with an intense expression, as if captivated by whatever she was saying. As I approached, she caught my eye.

"Oh, there she is. Quinn, this is Lennox and Zoe and Clark."

"Quinn and I had the pleasure of meeting this afternoon," Clark said. "If I remember correctly, you said you were looking forward to the complimentary rum punch being served tonight. Can I get you a glass?"

Nice of him to remember that detail. "Yes. Thank you." If he brought me a drink, I could trust it wasn't a figment of my imagination. The coffee table between us held glasses, napkins, coasters, and a flickering candle in the middle. Normal stuff. No random oil bottle illusions. Was it safe to assume it was only oil I had to be wary of? A muscle in my arm twitched.

"Anyone else?" Clark asked.

"I'll take another," said Lennox.

Zoe, a buxom auburn, waved him off. "These drinks are going straight to my head. I better take a break."

"Maybe one more," said Toni, to my surprise. "It's got an interesting smoky flavor, Quinn. I'm glad you're trying it. But I can't say it holds a candle to Quinn's concoctions," she said to the others. "What do you call someone who creates innovative, sophisticated drinks?"

"A mixologist?" Zoe suggested, leaning forward to scratch her ankle. When she nearly spilled out of her low-cut cocktail dress, I looked away and saw that Lennox kept his gaze on Toni.

"Toni's been telling us about your artisan café in Book-end Bay," Lennox said. "Ha! It rhymes. Did you do that on purpose, Quinn?"

The three of them laughed.

"Nope. Just a bonus, I guess." Apparently, I was behind as far as liquor consumption went.

"Well, Quinn's drinks are alcohol-free, so I don't know if mixologist is the right word," Toni said, then looked at me. "But you'd give the finest mixologist a run for her money." She patted my leg. A little too exuberantly. Was she trying to tell me something? She was hard to read because she was smiling at Lennox.

What was going on with her? She wasn't behaving as though he was our number one suspect.

"Quinn, you missed the announcement," Zoe said. "A glitch in Heart to Heart's system meant they couldn't announce who we'll be dating yet. I hope it's fixed soon." She smiled at Clark. He gave a non-committal nod I couldn't read. I wasn't feeling any great urgency to be matched with any of these men.

"I know who I'd like to date," said Lennox in a singsong voice, then he winked at Toni.

"Speaking of dating, Lennox," I said. "Toni told me you actually dated Alicia Smallwood last year," I said, watching for his reaction. He narrowed his gaze at me.

My comment also got Toni's attention. She glared at me, but I hoped she realized I was trying to keep to our objective, even if she'd come to a different conclusion about Lennox. This could be an opportunity to get further insight while Lennox was loosened up. *Stay with me, Toni.*

"Really?" Zoe said, crossing one leg over the other. "Isn't she the woman who drowned?"

"Yes," I confirmed. "She was one of the owners of Heart to Heart."

"What a horrible thing," Zoe said, looking at Lennox. "I'm sorry for your loss."

"It's okay," he said. "We broke up four months ago. I've moved on." He flashed Toni a tight smile.

"Still, it must have been sad, even if the relationship ended on bad terms," I said, hoping he would admit that it did.

The three of us looked at Lennox as he took a healthy gulp of his punch, then held onto the glass. "I wouldn't call it bad terms, and I don't want to come across as unfeeling, but I'm not grieving Alicia." He said it kindly.

"That must have been strange, though," Zoe said. "I don't think anyone's ever died after I broke up with them. You don't think she was despondent, do you?"

"For goodness' sake, no," said Lennox. "It was months ago. We'd *both* moved on."

"I have to agree with Zoe," I said. *Push him harder. Let's see if he has a short temper.* "It must feel a little strange if you were the one who ended things. Was it you who initiated the breakup, Lennox?" Nell had said that when Alicia ended the relationship, Lennox said she'd be sorry. I didn't have much of a history of breakups to relate to, but I knew people said things they didn't mean. Not that Lennox couldn't have acted on his threat.

Toni cleared her throat. "Alicia's death was a tragedy, but it doesn't sound like it had anything to do with their breakup." Her tone was confident. Maybe she'd learned something else about Lennox, or maybe she was trying to protect our cover.

Clark returned and handed me a tall glass. I paused to give Toni a chance to take over the conversation and for me to appreciate the punch. Even though she'd praised the drink, the deep, intense smoky flavor was a surprise and, as the name suggested, it packed a punch.

The sophisticated blend of liquors with rum undertone transported me to what I imagined being the heart of rum production in Havana. *Smooth.* If I were to drink these for the rest of the night, I'd have to crawl back to the room.

"That's right, Toni," Lennox said, taking a glass from Clark as he sat beside Zoe. "Not to speak ill of the dead, but Alicia Smallwood was too controlling for me. I like a strong-minded woman, but it was her way or the high-way."

"So you took the highway," Zoe said. "Cheers to that."

Hmm, not according to Nell. She said Alicia had insti-gated the breakup and Lennox said she'd be sorry for it. If that wasn't the case, then Lennox must have threatened her over something else.

You're getting nowhere. Change tactics. Maybe shar-ing a tidbit from my past could reveal whether Lennox had an alibi for the morning Alicia was killed. "I hear you, Lennox. I went through something similar during my marital breakup. My ex-husband's mistress was mur-dered."

"What!" Zoe said. "Holy cow, Quinn, that's crazy."

"The conversation sure took a turn while I was gone," Clark said.

The table went silent, everyone waiting for more. Toni stared at me with her head cocked.

I cleared my throat and continued. "It was also upset-ting because the police considered me as a suspect, but I had an air-tight alibi and they appeared to believe that I hadn't known about his affair before the woman was killed. Thank goodness."

"I would have been hysterical if that happened to me," said Zoe.

"It was pretty crazy. I wouldn't wish it on anyone. I sure hope you have an alibi for the night Alicia was killed, Lennox."

Everyone looked at him expectantly.

Lennox squirmed and gave a clipped laugh. "Her death was an accident, Quinn."

"I learned that someone close to Alicia isn't so sure and has convinced the police to look into it," I fabricated. "I'm just saying, after what happened to me, it would be good for you to have an alibi."

A look of shock crossed his face. *Ah, there it is. The exposed nerve.*

Chapter Eleven

"I DIDN'T KNOW THAT." He was quiet for a moment, but after his gaze darted between each one of us staring at him, he cleared his throat. "Well, um, let me think. It would have been...uh last Sunday morning." He paused, reflecting. "My son and I had a sunrise tee off. We golfed all morning. So, there's my alibi. Should the police come asking, I'm airtight." His smile looked forced to me.

"Where do you golf?" I asked. "I'm planning to take lessons this summer."

"I didn't know you were taking up golfing," Toni said. She seemed to be trying to make this difficult.

"Yes, I am. Lennox?"

"I'm a member of Green Glades," Lennox said.

Green Glades. I repeated this to myself a few times to get it into my memory. If I didn't reinforce a detail like this, it would get lost.

"You don't own gray gloves with orange strips on them, do you, Lennox?"

"What? No. Why are you asking me that?" He gave a nervous laugh and looked at Toni. "I think your friend is interrogating me."

Toni glared at me. "Quinn is an incredibly curious person."

Was she taking his side?

"Well, let's drink to curiosity not killing any cats," Zoe said, raising her glass.

"Cheers," I said. "And to Alicia." I tipped my glass toward Lennox.

He flushed and clinked my glass.

"Do you all want to know something juicy about Melody?" Zoe asked, fluffing her auburn curls.

Toni was right. I was a curious person, but I didn't encourage gossip, since it could spread like wildfire in a small town. People sometimes took it as gospel, forgetting the stories were rarely the whole truth. But in a situation like this, when we were trying to learn as many details as possible, gossip could be helpful. We'd verify details later.

I glanced at Toni, but she'd leaned into Lennox to listen to something he was saying quietly. *Toni!* I pressed into her leg with mine. She didn't move. *Fine. I'll do this myself.*

"Sure," I said to Zoe. "Spill the beans." I sat my glass on the table. As delicious as the punch was, I needed a clear mind to remember anything pertinent.

"Well, when I considered using a matchmaking service, I did some research first. I started with Cupid Connection. You know who they are, right? The competing matchmakers."

"That's right," Toni said, giving us her attention. Finally. "Who's the owner of Cupid Connection, Quinn?"

My jaw tightened. There was no reason for us to know anything about Cupid Connection. I caught her eye. *How much have you had to drink?* It had been a long time since I'd seen her like this. We didn't get carried away at a public event and not when we were supposed to be keeping our detecting undercover.

"Do you know Becca Brister?" Zoe asked.

"No, I don't," I said. "Like you, I did a little research before I signed up with Heart to Heart."

Toni hiccupped.

Zoe nodded in understanding. "Well, when I was at their office, I overheard Becca in an argument with our event planner, Melody Pennycook. Becca accused Melody of stealing a client list. Melody stormed out of there. She nearly knocked me over. I couldn't believe it when she introduced herself this morning."

Okay, this was a useful piece of information. Melody must have worked with Cupid Connection before working with Heart to Heart. Did this have any relevance to Alicia's death?

"I wonder if Melody is being sued for a breach of contract?" I asked. If that was the case, Alicia might have known it.

"Not necessarily," Clark said. "This isn't my area of expertise, but I believe it depends on whether Melody was a key employee at Cupid Connection. If she wasn't, then Becca couldn't stop Melody from offering her services to former clients. She has the right to make a living. But if Melody was considered a fiduciary of Cupid Connection, then she'd be obligated to act in the best interest of the company even if she left. In that case, she could not solicit her former employer's clients."

"I don't know anything about the matchmaking business, but I don't think Melody would have held that much weight," Zoe said. "I heard she's a freelancer."

"You know what I heard," Lennox said and paused for everyone to give him their attention.

Toni leaned closer to me. "I'm not feeling well."

Lennox looked at Toni. "I'd be happy to take you to your room, Toni."

Not a chance. "No, thank you," I snapped. No man we'd just met was going to take my drunken friend to her room. "We're staying together. I'll take Toni back to our room."

"Sorry you're not feeling well, Toni," Clark said.

Toni managed a smile.

"Don't you want to hear Lennox's gossip?" Zoe asked.

"What gossip?" Toni said, perking up.

Lennox sat up straighter. "Oh, well, it's not as interesting as Zoe's, but a few of the men are talking about one of the participants—a woman to stay away from."

"What? Why?" asked Zoe.

"Because she's been seen talking to herself—twice. Like a full-blown conversation. He says she's delusional, cuckoo, but I can't imagine they'd let someone like that into the event."

Holy crap. He's talking about me. And exaggerating. I have a reputation for cuckoo?

Toni looked at me with eyes a bit more sober all of a sudden.

"Oh, they probably included her on purpose," said Zoe. "You know how reality shows are. They like to have one wacko in the mix. Someone to create drama to keep the ratings up."

Cuckoo. Wacko. Suddenly, I wasn't feeling well either. But wait a minute. Just because I talked to dead people and had the odd hallucination didn't mean I was wacko. It meant I was special. I was having fantastical, enriching life experiences that the people in this room couldn't even imagine.

"We shouldn't judge anyone," I said. "You never know what's going on in someone's life." I picked up my purse. "Nice to chat with everyone. Let's go, Toni."

The next morning, when I knocked on Toni's bedroom door, she responded with a groan.

"Come in," called the frog in her throat. "I'm awake."

I opened the door, letting a burst of sunlight into the room. "How are we feeling this morning?"

Her eyes opened just a smidgen. She blocked the light with her hand. "Well, I no longer feel like I'm on the high seas, so that's an improvement."

Considering how she'd stumbled back to the room last night; I wasn't surprised things had been a little rocky. "You poor thing. I hope you don't feel too bad."

"What was in that rum punch last night?" she said, removing her hand and blinking. "I haven't been in a state like that since...I don't know. Maybe not since my wedding. I wasn't too annoying, was I?"

"You were more entertaining than you were annoying. I think you sang the full soundtrack from Sound of Music, but I fell asleep around My Favorite Things."

"Those are excellent songs."

"There's no denying that. And, Toni, don't blame yourself. The rum punch from last night was pure alcohol with a few liqueurs to sweeten it up and no more than a splash of juice."

"No kidding. I should have kept that in mind, but after half a glass, I was enjoying myself too much."

"I'm surprised the event would serve such a potent drink. Hopefully, things didn't get out of hand. I wonder if the breakfast buffet will include a side of headache medication."

"I took a couple last night." She flipped off the covers. "Do I smell coffee?"

"Yes. Coffee is made," I said, stepping back. "When you're up to it, I'd like to talk about our plan for today."

"Sure. Give me ten minutes."

While Toni used the bathroom, I looked up Green Glades Golf Course. I'd done some research and learned that Cupid Connection's event was taking place at an inn about an hour away. Since the golf course was in the same general direction, I figured we could visit both places today.

Looking somewhat refreshed, Toni poured herself a coffee, and I filled her in on Alec and the massage oil fiasco.

"I'm sorry this is happening to you," Toni said. "But do you really think these hallucinations are related to Alicia's death? I mean walnut oil, massage oil? Do you think they're clues?"

"I don't know how they could be, but we can keep them in mind whether they're related or not. It's just that the dream and the hallucinations started with Alicia's death."

"What do you think about seeing a psychic?" Toni suggested. "Maybe you can get an understanding of what's common as far as visions go."

She was right. I could use a mentor in all this and had to start somewhere. "That's not a bad idea. If the psychic is credible. When this is over, I'll call Colleen and get a referral." I added that to my to-do list. "I don't want to get side-tracked from why we're here since Nell is footing the bill. I looked up Cupid Connection and learned they're hosting their event this week at Lakeview Inn. According to Google Maps, the inn is about an hour away. I think we should get over there and talk to Becca Brister. Since she and Alicia were not on friendly terms, we should get a feel for how unfriendly. Maybe we can get someone to corroborate what Zoe said last night about Melody stealing a client list."

Toni screwed up her face. "Melody did what?"

"You don't remember that conversation?"

When she shook her head, I filled her in.

She looked sheepish. "Definitely avoiding the rum punch from now on. On a more pleasant note, I've been to Lakeview Inn. It's a beautiful place, and I'd love to visit again, but do you think Becca will have the time or willingness to talk to us when she's in the middle of this competition?"

"That's a good point." *I must visit Lakeview.* The urge to go to the inn settled in me like a clear, strong, irresistible compulsion. I wasn't sure if it was the voice of my intuition, but it felt important to follow through. I'd not received a push like this in a while. It was almost as if I was being guided. Could that be true? By whom? We were supposed to trust our inner voice, right? "My intuition says we should go anyway. I think we'll learn something useful at the inn."

"Okay. Then that's where we'll go."

I also wanted to know if she'd learned anything more about Lennox. At least I hoped she'd remember if she had. "Last night, did you notice Lennox told a different story about his breakup with Alicia? Nell said Lennox was angry over the breakup, but he made it sound as if it was his idea."

As she pondered that, her expression soured. "I remember you putting him on the spot, as if his breaking up with her was related to her death." Toni was getting defensive again.

"Well, that's what we're trying to figure out, right? If he wasn't angry at Alicia and didn't threaten her, then he may not have had a motive to kill her. Lennox said he had a golf game with his son that morning. We can try to verify that."

Toni's expression softened. "I don't think he's lying about it. I know you think I'm being foolish, but I have a good feeling about Lennox. When we talked about his relationship with Alicia, he had no bitterness toward her, not one bit."

Toni was a good judge of character, so I wasn't going to accuse her of misreading the situation. Not without proof, so hopefully we'd verify his alibi. I drained my coffee. "Okay. I'd like to get going. How much time do you need?"

"I'll be ready in twenty minutes." She picked up her coffee and took it into her bedroom.

While I waited, I sent Nell a text to tell her what we'd learned and what our plans were for the day. I also wanted to verify the Cupid Connection event's location.

Five minutes later, my phone rang. It was Nell.

"Hello, Quinn. Yes, you have the right location. I wanted to let you know I think Becca has been at it again. Someone spiked the rum punch last night. One of the bartenders found bottles of absinthe in the trash. It was 89% alcohol! Things could have gotten terribly out of hand if he hadn't stopped serving the punch. As it was, security had to get involved to break up more than one argument last night."

"Yikes." No wonder Toni had a headache this morning. It was a good thing we'd left the lounge when we did. I wondered if Moe could have been responsible for spiking the punch. It didn't seem to fit with his intention to bring cheer. "Do you have any proof it was someone from Becca's camp?"

"Not yet, but she's the one with the most to gain if we have fewer love matches. We both believe this television special could launch one of our businesses into the stratosphere, so there's a lot at stake. Please keep her underhanded ways in mind when you speak with her." *What does she expect us to do?* We had enough on our plate as it was, although I understood Nell's worry if someone was trying to sabotage her event. Should I burden her further with the gossip I'd heard about Melody? What if it wasn't true? Before I'd decided, she started talking.

"Quinn, there's something I need to talk to you about. It's awkward." Her tone was slightly cooler.

I didn't like awkward. "Oh? What is it?"

"Courtney was inputting the data from the profile forms you and Toni filled in, and she said...well—"

Cripes! Brielle had been unsuccessful in retrieving those things. "I'm sorry, Nell," I interrupted. "Toni and I were being silly. Those forms were *not* supposed to be handed in. The cleaners must have taken them from our room."

"The cleaners wouldn't do that. When Courtney brought them to my attention, I said you surely meant them as a joke. She didn't think they were funny, more on the side of disrespectful, considering you're a friend of mine, so I had to do some quick talking to reassure her you and Toni are sincere in this endeavor."

I sighed. "I'm really sorry. We didn't mean to be disrespectful. I'll talk to Courtney and explain we were off our heads or something."

"I'd appreciate that. It might help smooth things over, so she's not wondering why you're here."

"Okay. I'll take care of it. Sorry, Nell."

"It's okay, Quinn. I can laugh about it."

I hung up, feeling foolish and embarrassed. As a business owner myself, I could relate to Nell being sensitive about my mocking her profile questions. Sometimes, it was hard to separate the business from the person. I still had a difficult time not taking it personally when one of my customers didn't like our featured scone or signature drink. When someone left a nasty review calling our verb of the month juvenile, I'd let it get to me and had considered ending it. Then Poppy pointed out that we were not catering to the few who didn't enjoy our theme, but to the many who did. It's impossible to please everyone.

As I remembered these things, I felt doubly bad about the profiles. I didn't want to be thought of as a nasty critic. At the same time, Toni and I hadn't meant any harm and certainly hadn't intended for those forms to be handed in. Could housekeeping have been responsible for that? How else could the profiles have gotten into Courtney's hands? I wondered about a certain ghost clown. I guess it didn't really matter. The damage was done. Hopefully, I'd make it up to Nell by finding the truth behind Alicia's death.

Chapter Twelve

"Nope, there's no record of Lennox Huff or his son teeing off at sunrise last Sunday," said the freckle-faced guy staffing the shop at Green Glades Golf Course. He registered golfers and managed tee times. Toni had told him her boyfriend Lennox's son had borrowed her nine iron, then left it behind at the club.

"Are you absolutely sure?" she asked. "Maybe it wasn't that morning, or maybe he and his son played later in the day?"

"I know all the members by name here at Green Glades, and I've never seen Mr. Huff play with his son. I didn't even know he had a son."

"Well, that doesn't make sense," Toni said.

The guy shrugged. "You asked. I'm telling you what I know. That's all." He set the mouse aside. "Anything else?"

"No, thank you," I said. "You've been very helpful."

"Lennox lied, Toni," I said as we walked out the door. I didn't enjoy seeing the disappointment on Toni's face, but I was glad we'd caught Lennox in a lie before Toni was further invested.

"I realize that, but I don't understand it." Toni slid her sunglasses onto her face from the top of her head. "Geez, it's bright out here."

"It doesn't mean he killed Alicia, but that he made up an alibi doesn't look good."

"Well, Quinn, it's not like you had the authority to interrogate him. He wasn't obligated to tell the truth. Maybe he was home alone but wanted to say something to end the conversation. Or he might have gotten mixed up, or he was drunk. Nell did say someone spiked the punch."

I got in the truck and waited until Toni was inside. "Yeah, maybe. But there's no need to make excuses for him."

"I'm not making excuses. I'm just looking at this from all sides. We're taking that guy's word over Lennox's. I want us to keep that in mind as well."

I gave her a look. "I can't imagine why that guy would lie about Lennox playing golf. You obviously like Lennox. Are you seeing him through impartial eyes?"

She gave me a look right back. "Of course, my eyes are impartial, and yes, I like Lennox. What are you suggesting?"

I started the truck. "You seem to be on the defensive when it comes to Lennox, that's all."

She was quiet for a little while. "When Lennox and I first started chatting, he said this thing that Norman said during our first conversation—so, tell me, Toni, what makes you tick? No one, besides Norman, has ever asked me that, and...well, Lennox sparked a nice memory."

Any frustration I felt toward Toni disintegrated. She'd adored her husband Norman, and I understood why she'd be attracted to a man who reminded her of him. "Oh, Toni. If you like this man, then we better prove he's innocent."

"I appreciate that, although I'm okay if things don't go any further with Lennox. I've had a nice time chatting with him, but he's no Norman."

"No man will ever be," I said. Last year she'd admitted that since Norman died, she'd put him high on a pedestal, until no one could ever compare to her late husband—not even possibly the real Norman, who'd been a wonderful man, but not perfection. She was having a difficult time letting any man get close. Now, I wanted Lennox to be a good guy. For Toni's sake. But something wasn't right, so we'd have to do more digging. Maybe we'd get answers at the Cupid Connection event. At least I hoped the visit wouldn't be a waste of time.

An hour later, we arrived at Lakeview Inn. After parking the truck, I noticed I'd received a text from Alec. *Hope you're keeping warm and having a fantastic day. Looking forward to our date.*

Our date. He was calling it a date, not just dinner. Was that because I was attending a matchmaking event, and he was concerned my undercover dating would have me falling for someone? Meanwhile, I still wasn't sure I wanted to change my life, especially when my life was so weird. *When would I know?* My thoughts were too scattered to think about it. I sent Alec a quick reply, telling him I was also looking forward to dinner and wished him a wonderful day as well. Then I put my phone away and caught up to Toni.

Where the Great Bear Resort was all wood and stone, Lakeview had the look of a French chateau with stone cladding, detailed dormer windows, and a steeply pitched roof with many massive chimneys.

"This isn't too shabby," I said.

"It's a nice place all right. Norman and I stayed here for our twentieth wedding anniversary. I'd call it old world elegance. I specifically remember having my first Baked Alaska here."

"I don't think I've ever had Baked Alaska. Is that the baked ice cream flambé?"

Toni licked her lips. "Yes. It was all very dramatic to have your dessert set on fire. And now that I think of it, I've never had it since."

As we entered the inn, I crossed my fingers that we'd learn something valuable. At the reception desk, Toni asked where to find Becca Brister.

"She's sitting right over there," the clerk said, pointing to three people clustered around a coffee table.

"Which one is Becca?" Toni asked.

"She's the one in the white jacket." A heavy-set woman with chin-length, blue-grey hair cut in a straight bob was deep in conversation.

"Thank you," I said as we stepped away. "We'll have to wait until she's free. Shall we sit over there?" As I motioned toward a couple of chairs, the hallway beyond the reception area drew my attention. An urge struck me to continue down the hall. Actually, it was stronger than an urge. It was almost as if I was a magnet being drawn to true north. Something was down there that I needed to see. "Do you mind waiting here for Becca while I check out the rooms down there?"

Toni looked at me questioningly. "Down where?"

"Just down the hall. I'll fill you in later."

"Okay, but hurry. Becca could be free at any moment."

"Thanks. I won't be long." As I headed down the hall toward a display sign, the hum of a large group of people grew louder as I reached an open double door. It looked like a convention—booths and aisles and lots of people. The sign outside the door read Superior Psychic Expo featuring professional psychic readers, mediums, palmists, psychic healing, reiki, spirit communication and more.

Toni and I had just talked about psychics, and now I'd been drawn down this hallway to a psychic expo. I was meant to be here.

Snagging a brochure, I read that for five dollars, I could browse over seventy booths and take part in a dozen workshops. I didn't have time for any of that. I'd have to come back with Toni after we talked to Becca. But as I read further, I saw the fair was ending at noon today. I checked my watch. Twenty minutes from now. I quickly paid the entrance fee and hoped that whatever guiding force brought me here had a plan, and I'd feel drawn to someone who could tell me if my hallucinations were common for psychic-like people. I could get their business card and connect later.

A bit overwhelmed by the number of people, I stood for a moment taking it all in. One booth had a few folks laying on cots receiving a free reiki treatment. Next to them, a man hung out in front of a table with bottles of colored liquids he apparently used to balance chakras. Maybe I was suffering a serious imbalance, although I didn't feel drawn to him. Surely I was meant to connect with someone here. I passed booths selling walking sticks, crystals, tarot decks, aura photography. Oh, wait. Aura photography. I'd forgotten about auras. A couple of years ago, before I met Brielle, a ghost told me I had two auras. Maybe I should grab a card from this booth.

"It's a lot to take in, isn't it?" said a woman standing beside me. Her silver hair was pulled back, revealing purple crystal wings dangling from her ears. It was difficult to determine her age since her face had hardly a wrinkle, but her silver hair looked natural. Her irises were nearly as dark as her pupils, or perhaps it was the dim room creating an illusion.

"It really is," I said. Wait a minute. Where did I know this woman from? "You look familiar. Have we met?"

She stared at me, tilted her head. "Have we?"

Then it came to me. "Were you in the grocery store in Bookend Bay?"

"Oh, probably. I've been in there twice picking up supplies." She had a warm, friendly demeanor.

That's where I knew her from. She'd been in the aisle when I'd seen the broken bottle of walnut oil. Should I ask her if she'd seen it or would that just sound weird?

"I've never been to a psychic fair before," she said, almost apologetically.

"Me neither. I don't know where to start." Not to mention, I was trying to take it all in super fast.

"I'm not even sure this is where I need to be," she said.

Hmm, that was an interesting thing to say since in a way I felt the same. I didn't know if any of these practitioners could help me or how to find one who could. The urge I'd felt earlier was gone. So far, I'd not seen any booths boasting help with hallucinations or parallel universe visitors. I kept this to myself, though. The thought of sharing my personal oddities with a stranger made me uncomfortable. Still, there was something about this woman, an openness perhaps, that made her easy to talk to.

"This probably sounds strange," she said. "But it's serendipitous that I'm here today."

Okay, that got my attention. "I feel the same. I came to the inn for a reason unrelated to this psychic fair. As a matter of fact, I left my friend in the lobby because I felt compelled to see what was going on down the hall. That's how I found this."

She cocked her head, penetrating my eyes with her gaze. "Interesting. I had a similar experience. I'm Adelaide, by the way," she said, offering her hand.

"It's nice to meet you. I'm Quinn."

When she took my hand, she stood up straighter, tilted her head, and stared deeply into my eyes for a few seconds. Her expression turned quizzical, then she let go, looked away for a moment, then back and gave her head a shake.

Why was she looking at me that way?

"Sorry, I got distracted for a moment," she said. "Anyway, I'm here because a couple of days ago, I got the urge to call an old friend of mine. Her name just popped into my mind. That kind of thing happens to everyone, right?"

"Yes. Those things are normal. I've had similar experiences." I had the feeling she wanted reassurance. Unless she meant something else. Something stronger, like the compulsion I'd experienced, or possibly something to do with whatever had distracted her.

"What I meant by serendipitous is that this friend of mine, who lives clear across the country, was supposed to be staying at this inn today. I'm from the south. I've just inherited a sailboat, so I also had a reason to be in Michigan today, too. Strange, huh? We made a plan to meet for lunch. Imagine both of us being in Upper Michigan at the same time."

I was anxious about Toni waiting, so I nudged Adelaide to the next booth. "It's nice when the stars align like that." And not as unusual as what I was dealing with.

"Just as I pulled into the parking lot, I received a text from her saying her flight got diverted to Chicago, and she wouldn't arrive until dinner time. So now I've got a free afternoon—hence the psychic fair."

It didn't sound like she'd been drawn to the psychic fair like I'd been.

"That's not why you're here." This came from a woman clad in white standing under a sign that said Masters of Elven Enchantments and Faerie Light.

"Are you speaking to me?" Adelaide asked.

The woman's assessing gaze passed over both of us. "I'll address you both, since you've come for guidance."

That also got my attention.

"I'm Kya," the woman in white said. Intelligent hazel eyes welcomed us. She had a pale complexion and black hair cut in an asymmetrical bob, shoulder length on one side and chin length on the other. "Tell me your names."

Adelaide introduced herself as she touched her dangling earring.

I suddenly wondered if they represented faery wings, and this had prompted Kya to call out to us.

"And I'm Quinn."

"You are sisters," Kya said.

"No," I said. "We just met five minutes ago."

She smiled as if she knew a secret. "That doesn't matter. You belong to the sisterhood. I mean the greater sisterhood. The faeries and elves have always had a kinship with witches and all magical practitioners, especially healers." Her gaze pierced Adelaide on this last word.

Adelaide laughed. "I'm afraid I'm no healer. If anything, I'm having the opposite effect on people. Not that people are falling ill—I don't mean that. What's happening is just...weird."

Kya nodded, knowingly. "I'm not surprised."

Really? She knew what Adelaide was talking about?

By the quizzical look on Adelaide's face, she must have been thinking the same thing. "Why do you say that?"

"Because from what I feel coming from you, your powers are a mess. Don't take that personally. It's common for novices. I believe in being direct, so I'll tell you what I feel as an intuitive. Your energy is too frenetic for you to control it, so it's no wonder *weird* things are happening."

Weird things were happening to me, too. "What can she do about this frenetic energy?" I asked.

Kya turned her attention to me. Instead of looking me in the eye, she appeared to be looking around me. Her expression turned quizzical. "Your third eye is wide open, but...there's something else going on. I can't figure you out, so hold on for a second." She looked at Adelaide. "How much do you know about magic?"

Magic? Could Kya be picking up my alternate? I pictured Brielle, on a broom, flying from her dimension into mine.

My phone rang. If Toni wasn't waiting for me, I wouldn't have answered, but that wouldn't be fair to her. Reluctantly, I stepped away.

Sure enough, it was Toni.

"She's free," Toni said. "I'm going to grab her now before she gets away. Hurry!" The phone went dead.

I couldn't leave without getting Adelaide's contact information—that felt right to me—so I quickly joined the two women. Kya was talking about enchantments to Adelaide who looked like she'd rather be anywhere else. I knew that feeling as the familiar tug-of-war occurred inside me. How did conversations about enchantments become part of my life? But I needed to trust that something drew me here for a reason, because I didn't know where else to go for answers.

"I'm sorry to interrupt, but I have to leave," I said. "Could we exchange contact information, Adelaide? Kya?"

"Absolutely," Adelaide said. "I'd like to talk further. My boat is in a little town called Bookend Bay, so I'm staying there."

Another coincidence? "I know it well," I said. "I live in Bookend Bay."

"I can give you my business card," Kya said, offering it to me from her pocket. "I might be able to help calm things down for you, too, but unfortunately I'll be in Europe for the next three months."

That was disappointing. I wanted to know more about what it meant to be an intuitive. I took the card. "Thanks, Kya."

Adelaide and I added each others' contact details to our phones.

"I'm sorry. I really have to go. I'll text you later." I wanted to speak more with Adelaide and learn more about the weird things happening in her life. I also wanted to know what she learned from Kya. Didn't it just figure I was leaving this event with more questions than answers? Seemed to be the story of my life.

Chapter Thirteen

"Here she is," Toni said loudly as I scooted down the hall to join her and Becca. "Quinn, this is Becca Brister."

"It's nice to meet you." I shook her hand, trying to get my mind off intuitive powers and enchantments and back on the murder case.

Toni's expression was rather serious. "I was just explaining to Becca that we're from the contest committee, here to investigate the complaint filed by a contestant."

Good one, Toni! I gave a sympathetic look and nodded as if it was difficult delivering unpleasant, yet official, contest business.

"It's a shame Heart to Heart's event turned into a drunkfest," Becca said, with no trace of sympathy. "I wish I was responsible for it, but I had nothing to do with spiking anyone's rum punch."

Becca wasn't trying to hide her bitterness and obviously had hard feelings toward Heart to Heart. If she believed we were from the contest committee, why not behave professionally? Why admit she wasn't above trying to derail her competitor? It made me think she had spiked the punch. I didn't think Moe was responsible. It didn't fit his modus operandi. Drunk people did foolish things. Someone could have gotten hurt.

"If anyone should complain, it's me," Becca said. "Alicia Smallwood started the bad blood between us by maligning Cupid Connection on social media. She said we allowed a breach in our system that exposed the personal details of our clients to the public. That was an outright lie."

It also sounded a lot like the story Melody told, but she'd said it was the other way around. Maybe Alicia and Becca had attacked each other's company on social media.

Too bad I didn't have a lie detector. Could an intuitive like Kya sense if someone was telling the truth? Could I? Maybe an untapped power like that resided inside me. I could only hope.

"Are you talking about the alleged theft of your client list by Melody...er...I can't remember her last name," Toni asked.

"Melody Pennycook," Becca supplied. "Yes, that's exactly what I'm talking about. Alicia should have fired that crook for it, but instead she used the information to steal our clients and make us look bad. Alicia Smallwood was a..." She left this hanging, but it didn't take an intuitive to extrapolate.

So it sounded like Melody did indeed steal Becca's client list. Maybe this led to the bitterness between Becca and Alicia, or maybe those seeds were sown earlier. If Becca believed Alicia was behind the client list theft and had then used it to malign Becca's company, could

Becca have been angry enough to kill Alicia for it? *Another suspect.*

I studied Becca, dropping my gaze to her hands—large hands. Strong hands? Becca had at least fifty pounds on Alicia. Was that enough to have overpowered her in a fight to the death? As I watched Becca, I tuned into everything I was feeling, but instead of clarity, discomfort settled inside me. *Why is that?* I looked away, not understanding what was going on inside me. Nothing was clear, but maybe whatever characteristic gave someone the propensity to murder, also gave them the skill to cover it up, and I'd been delusional thinking I'd receive a psychic message identifying a killer.

"Did Melody have anything against Alicia?" Toni asked, doing a great job. "It seems like this list stealing has led to both your events being sabotaged."

"Not that I know of," Becca said. "But I wouldn't have put it past Alicia to have tried to pilfer my clients. Melody and Alicia were probably thick as thieves."

"Did this animosity between you and Alicia start with the stolen client list?" I asked.

"Gosh no. Do you know the first time I met Alicia, she said it was apparent I wasn't overburdened by my education?"

"Ouch," said Toni.

Typical Alicia.

The sound of distant screams interrupted our conversation.

"Good grief! What's going on?" I asked.

Becca had already started running toward the screams. Toni and I looked at each other and followed Becca down the hall. People streamed from a doorway. Everyone was soaking wet.

"What happened?" Becca asked.

"The sprinkler system turned on!" someone cried.

One soggy woman with drenched hair and murder in her eyes stormed past us, calling for maintenance.

"I'm wearing cashmere!" said a man, shaking the bottom of his sweater.

Another woman nearly slipped as she ran from the room.

"Just calm down, everyone," Becca yelled, waving her arms.

"Calm down? This is a nightmare," a woman said, holding onto her friend. Behind them, a man was having a good laugh.

"I meant be careful," Becca ordered. "The floor is wet. How could something like this happen?"

These people must be from Becca's matchmaking event. Some were wetter than others, but everyone was smartly dressed and not sticking around to find out what caused the downpour.

Becca took off toward reception. Toni and I stuck our heads in the ballroom. Water was still spraying down from the overhead sprinklers, soaking tables, chairs, and everything left behind. *What a disaster.*

"I wonder what could have caused the sprinkler to go off?" Toni asked.

"Or who?"

"Oh dear, do you think Heart to Heart's prankster has branched out?" she asked.

"Maybe retaliated, since these two matchmakers seem to be attacking each other."

Toni nodded. "I hope it doesn't escalate."

Three maintenance staff came running down the hall. Toni and I stepped back to let them do their thing. "Let's get going. I'd like to stop at Break Thyme before we get back to the resort."

"Yes, let's do that. I received a message to say the courier delivered my package. I can't wait to show you what I bought."

Uh oh. Lately, Toni had been spending a lot on Break Thyme, and she refused to let me reimburse her. She had excellent taste, so everything she chose was lovely, but I couldn't afford to spend money like she did and I didn't want to take advantage of her. "Toni, you're not supposed to be spending your money on Break Thyme."

"Never you mind. I told you it makes me happy. You know I have more money than I need."

"I'm glad your investments have done so well." As we reached my truck, I noticed a man getting into a car across from us. We made eye contact and before my brain could place him, he was inside his car. Where did I know him from? And then I remembered—the tech guy who'd fixed the debit machine when Toni and I were registering at Great Bear—Courtney's fiancée, Dario.

"Toni, look at that silver car over there. Can you see the man inside?" The car started and backed out of its spot, but the angle was such that his face wasn't visible. He shot out of the parking lot.

"No. I couldn't see him. Why?"

"I think it was the tech guy we met when we registered. His name is Dario. You remember—Courtney's fiancée."

"Yes, I remember him. What would he be doing here?"

"That's what I'm wondering."

"Hmm. You don't suppose he had anything to do with the sprinkler going off?" Toni asked.

"We can't make any assumptions, but the timing is suspicious."

I unlocked the truck, and we got inside. "If Dario is responsible for this stunt, then what does he gain by sabotaging Heart to Heart's competitor?"

"Could be money," Toni said. "If Heart to Heart wins the competition, maybe there's an opportunity for Dario to get involved in the project."

Possible. "It's a lot easier to get a job when you have a connection or know someone."

As I started the truck, I caught sight of a green bottle in my cup holder. *What was that?*

"That's for sure," Toni said. "He's getting married, so he'll have extra expenses."

I didn't remember putting that bottle in my cup holder. My nerves turned on edge. *Is that real?* I stared at the bottle, wondering if it would be gone the next time I looked.

"My friend Grace's daughter spent over forty thousand on her wedding," Toni said. "Can you believe it? Quinn?" Toni said.

Is that bottle an illusion? I reached for it tentatively with my index finger to give it a poke, as if it might bite me. My finger bounced off. It was solid.

"What are you doing?" Toni asked. "Help yourself. It's great hand lotion."

"Oh, it's yours." Relief settled my nerves.

"Who did you think it belonged to?"

"Never mind. Thanks, but I'm good." I backed out of the parking space and headed to Break Thyme.

We talked about the case a little more, agreeing that we had reasons to suspect Becca because of her hatred of Alicia. Lennox appeared to have lied about his golf game with his son, meaning he not only had no alibi for the morning Alicia was killed, but he may also have tried to fabricate one. Melody had a black mark against her for stealing her employer's client list, but so far, we'd not discovered a motive for murder. Same with Dario. He might be guilty of vandalism, but we had no reason to suspect him of murder.

I told Toni about the psychic fair and meeting Kya and Adelaide. I wanted to talk with them both again and learn more about the magic Kya had referenced. I didn't think she was referring to spells and potions, but she might have meant the power to control the energy I might possess because whatever was happening to me, I needed to get this under control.

"They're perfect!" Toni exclaimed, as she opened the box that had come in the mail. "Exactly what I'd pictured." She held up the cookie jar, a turquoise sea glass color with rope coiled around the mouth of the jar and a knobby piece of driftwood fixed to the lid.

Poppy removed a second jar, green sea glass with coral fixed to the lid. "They're beautiful, Toni. They'll look great on the counter. You've got a beachy theme going on here now, and it's classy, not overdone."

"I love them," I said, removing a sky-blue jar. "And I agree with Poppy. I love the beachy vibe." It made sense since Break Thyme was on the lake by a sandy beach. I didn't have the patience to pull a theme together, not like Toni did. She'd purchased elegant white platters with silver paddle handles to display our packaged cookies. Etched glass lanterns adorned the patio tables outside, although it was too cold for people to sit outside today.

"Well, thank you very much," Toni said, setting the jar by the sink. "I'll get these washed. What else needs to be done, Poppy?"

"Ivy and I have everything under control," she said.

"That's great, so I can get paperwork done," I said, thinking about the accounting I needed to stay on top of before it got overwhelming. "Toni, can you give me an hour and then we'll head back to the resort?"

"That's fine with me," she said.

Poppy took a carton of cream from the fridge. "I'm going to top up the cream, then I want to hear all about your case, Toni."

I went upstairs to my office, which I still thought of as my office even though it had become my living space. As I worked, I kept expecting to look up and see Brielle, but she didn't show up. When everything was up to date, Toni and I drove back to Great Bear Resort in time for dinner.

People were lined up to get into the dining room. From the windbreakers and polo shirts, it looked like Great Bear's golf course had had a busy day. Toni and I joined the line and were chatting with the woman ahead of us when Lennox approached.

"If it isn't my favorite person," Lennox said, gaze on Toni. "I've been looking for you all afternoon."

Toni's smile wasn't as warm as it had been yesterday. "Duty called," she said, not elaborating.

"Ooh, I like a driven woman." He winked at her, then looked at me. "So, do you think there's a good chance Toni picked me for her first date? They're going to announce the matches tonight. I'm keeping my fingers crossed." He hadn't picked up on Toni's cool vibe—one I could have sensed from ten feet away.

"I'm not giving anything away," I said, trying to remember my choices for a one-on-one date. I wasn't that keen on any of the men I'd met. I wondered what Alec was doing tonight.

"Ah, you're a tough nut to crack," said Lennox, stroking his chin, gaze on Toni. "One woman I spoke with, and I'm not naming names, said she couldn't have a relationship with any man who didn't share the same style of dress as her." He leaned back, put out his hands, and looked down at his navy button-down shirt and tan pants. "Do you think I made the cut?"

"You look fine," she said.

"I guess I'll take that positively. Honestly, I thought she was kidding, so I laughed, but I shouldn't have. She was serious."

"You can't fault someone for being honest," Toni said, then she poked the woman ahead of us. "Would you like to join Quinn and I for dinner?"

"Yes," she said, fluffing her blonde hair. "Thank you. I'm pushing myself outside my comfort zone with this entire event. I don't know what I was thinking. I'm terribly introverted."

"Good for you," Lennox said. "I think it's admirable to push yourself. And I'd love to share a table with you all."

The hostess interrupted before we could object. I knew Toni was too kind to tell Lennox she'd rather not sit together. Reading her body language told me that much, but I didn't know how to convey it without being rude, so I followed the hostess to our table.

"Aren't I lucky to have the company of three lovely women?" Lennox said, pulling Toni's chair out. I had to give him credit for being a gentleman.

"Lennox?" A woman, passing by our table, stopped and stared at him. "What are you doing here? I thought you must have been in a car accident or something. Were you playing golf today?"

Lennox flushed red and gave a nervous chuckle. "Hello, Darla. No. No, nothing like that. I'm just catching up with friends." *Interesting.* I wouldn't call us friends.

With a quizzical expression, Darla looked at the three of us, then back to Lennox. "Why haven't you responded to my messages? Nothing since last Monday morning. We had that glorious weekend together, and you ghosted me!"

Lennox swallowed. "I'm sorry, Darla. Can I call you later, and we can talk then?"

Call back later? I take back my gentleman assessment.

She folded her arms over her chest. "Don't tell me you're part of this matchmaking event, Lennox, cause if you are..."

This was getting worse. The four of us looked at Lennox.

"Uh—well—er..." he stammered. "Let's talk about this outside." He tried to take her hand, but she whipped it away from him.

"Why? Because you don't want your friends to know what a scumbag you are. I don't believe it. What a fool I've been, worrying about you. I even went to your house, knocking on the doors, peering in the windows to see if you'd fallen and hurt yourself. I thought you were the man of my dreams."

Toni's eyes had grown wide. She blinked. "You were in a relationship as of last weekend?"

"Yes, he was!" Darla said. "We've been together for two months. Spent the entire weekend together in Minneapolis. He dropped me off at work on Monday morning, and that's the last I heard from him."

Wait a minute. If Lennox was with Darla last weekend, then he couldn't have killed Alicia. He made up the excuse about the golf game to hide the fact he'd been in a relationship, not to give himself an alibi.

"Listen, Darla. I should have been honest with you," he said. "I knew things weren't working out. I never should have agreed to go away last weekend."

Poor Darla. Her bottom lip quivered. She shook her head, turned, and hurried from the restaurant.

"You better go after her," Toni said sternly to Lennox. "And keep going."

Chapter Fourteen

THE NEXT MORNING BRIELLE arrived and immediately told me that in her life, she'd nodded off after a morning of love-making with Julien. I wondered if her work was suffering, but it wasn't my job to manage her life.

We set out on a walk along a trail at the resort. Since anyone watching wouldn't see my invisible twin, I wore ear buds to feign a phone conversation and tried not to look at her while she talked about her ex-husband.

"My marriage didn't break down because of one thing," Brielle said. "But a major problem was our different levels of intelligence. I'm a curious person and want to learn new things. My ex did not. He was perfectly happy to keep things exactly as they were. He had no interest in exploring new opportunities or learning new skills."

We certainly had our curious natures in common. "My ex was like that, too. His idea of fun was to sit in front of the television and watch sports, glued to the TV every night. Drove me crazy. I wanted to travel, but he didn't like the idea of leaving the country."

"You stayed with him a long time, Quinn. That must have been difficult."

"I wanted to keep my family together for the kids. When they moved out, I desperately needed something more, a challenge. That was why I wanted to open a café."

"I'm happy you made that happen. Do you have any travel plans?"

"Not at the moment. I met a woman yesterday who just inherited a sailboat. I've always loved the water. Doesn't it sound romantic to see the world from a sailboat?"

She grabbed my arm. "Holy cow. If that isn't kismet, I don't know what is. Julien owns a sailboat. He wants us to sail the Mediterranean together. I'm so excited about it, I just signed myself up for sailing lessons."

Envy slithered up my spine, and I wasn't proud of it. I often found myself emotionally uncomfortable with Brielle. She was literally living the life I didn't choose, so when hers looked better than mine, I felt like kicking myself. But I had to remind myself that wasn't reasonable. The most important things in my life were my kids and Gabriel, and I wouldn't have them if I'd chosen her life. But she was getting to sail the Mediterranean with a sexy Frenchman. It was hard not to hanker for a little of that.

"You're going to have an amazing time." I checked my watch. I was supposed to meet Toni in twenty-five minutes to find out who we'd been matched with for our dates this afternoon. Maybe I could have fun with this experience. There was no sense bemoaning Brielle's romance if I wasn't willing to put myself out there. Otherwise, I was guaranteed not to find my Julien, not that I wanted a Julien. *Did I?* Maybe my indecision meant it wasn't time to make a life change. I couldn't resolve this quandary right now. "We need to turn around now because I have to get back."

I told Brielle about the psychic fair and meeting Adelaide and Kya. "A few things interested me. First, Kya called herself an intuitive. I'm wondering if I have this ability, too. She also said my third eye is wide open, whatever that means. Do you think that's why I'm hallucinating? Has anything like this happened to you?"

"Not like that, no. Why oils?"

"Let's think about this for a moment," I said. "What does oil symbolize?"

"Look it up on your phone."

I pulled out my phone and typed the question into the search bar. "There's nothing about walnut oil. It says here that *olive* oil symbolizes light and knowledge, a source of enlightenment."

"Enlightenment, huh? That sounds like it might relate to your third eye."

"It just figures the path to my enlightenment is found in a broken bottle of oil in the spice aisle. The broken part makes sense, considering how bizarre my life is, but enlightened? I feel anything but enlightened."

"Well, it's probably a long and winding path," she said with a chuckle. "Perhaps Kya will have some answers. Or the sailboat woman, Adelaide. She said weird things were happening to her. I've been popping into Break Thyme at night. Do you want me to poke around in her boat?"

We'd justified using Brielle's unique qualities to help solve murders, but poking into a woman's private life, which may or may not be helpful, didn't feel justified. "No.

I don't think we have the right to do that. Besides, I don't know which boat is hers, and I doubt she's staying on the boat. It didn't sound like she had any experience with them."

"Okay, then. Hands off Adelaide."

As we reached the end of the trail, the smell of campfires wafted our way. "I'm going to say goodbye now. Have fun with your sailing lessons."

"Thanks, and you have fun with your date. It's with Alec, right?"

"No. I've been set up with someone from the event."

"Oh," she said, sounding disappointed. "I think Alec is the right man for you. Can you not give him a chance?"

"I never said I wouldn't give him a chance. I'm having dinner with him when the event is over."

"Good, good. I find it interesting that we both married similar men, then as we learned more about ourselves, we realized we weren't compatible with our husbands. I needed more life experience to really get to know myself before knowing what I wanted in a partner. I waited a long time for someone like Julien, and even though our relationship is new, I can already see the rest of my life with him. He's so easy to be around, and I can tell him exactly what's on my mind and he listens."

"Are you going to tell him about your visits to my life?"

She winced. "I don't think we're ready for that just yet."

"I understand it's an uncomfortable conversation to have, but it's important to know if he believes you."

"I'll think about it," she said.

We were quiet for a minute, then she said, "Alec reminds me of Julien, you know. I believe he's a man who will feed your curious nature, not stymie it like your ex did. He's also independent and won't expect you to look after him. He reads. He cooks, and he keeps a clean house."

"He keeps a clean house? How do you know so much about Alec?"

"You know me. I've been watching."

Oh boy. So, she had invaded Alec's privacy. It was difficult for me to criticize her since I wasn't sure I'd be able to resist doing the same if the tables were turned. It killed me not to ask her to tell me more, everything she'd learned about him, but I didn't have time. For now, I had to be satisfied she'd seen nothing to deter me from Alec. It was truly remarkable to have the perspective of another me. Maybe if we pooled our learning experiences, we'd be twice as wise one day. "Oh, Brielle." I just shook my head. "Now, I've really got to go."

"Do you know who they matched you with?" I asked Toni when I caught up with her in the lounge.

"We should get a text any minute," she said. "Lennox messaged me to say he left the resort for good, so he's out of the picture. Who would you want to go on a date with?"

I wiggled my head in uncertainty. "I've been so distracted since I got here, I can hardly remember who's who. The only guy I'd think I'd like to get to know is the lawyer—Clark."

"The estate lawyer from the other night?"

"Yes, that Clark."

"I didn't realize you'd spoken to him earlier. I put him down as one of my choices."

"Oh, I didn't know you'd spoken to him, either. Well, don't worry about it. I'm not set on anyone." *Except maybe Alec, after what Brielle said.*

Toni's phone chimed. She read the text, then gave me a sheepish look.

"You've been matched with Clark," I guessed.

"Yes. I'm sorry. Should I—"

"Go on your date? Yes. Go. Have fun."

Her smile held excitement. "I'm going on a date. An official date. Can you believe it?"

I could actually. She seemed ready for this. I'd never seen Toni eager to meet a man. "Yes, I can! I hope you have a fabulous time."

"Me too. But what if I don't like him? What do I do?"

"If that happens, and I doubt it will, it's only one afternoon. He'd have to be pretty bad to not be able to stand his company for a few hours."

"Right," Toni said, digging through her purse. "Did you get a message yet?"

I looked at my screen. "Not yet."

Toni reapplied her lipstick. "I want to hear who you're matched with before I go."

As I combed through my memory, the men I'd chosen came back to me. "I think it could be Mac or Gregory, unless they didn't write my name down for a date."

"I didn't talk to Gregory."

"I imagine I'll be matched with Mac. Now that I recall, he said he'd like to talk again." My phone chimed. "Ah, the message has arrived." I looked to see I'd have my one-on-one date with a man I didn't recognize. "It says I've been matched with Bernardo. I don't remember talking to a Bernardo." I guessed that meant Mac hadn't chosen me after all. Perhaps he'd had a stronger connection with someone else, like all the men I'd spoken with since I'd not been matched with any of them.

"This could be good," Toni said, fluffing her hair. "It must mean the matchmakers think you and Bernardo will be ideal together."

"Maybe. It says I'm supposed to meet him at the pool."

"Fun. I'm supposed to meet Clark at the stables. I haven't been horseback riding in years. It's bound to be an adventure. I'm going to go now." Toni gave me a hug. "Have a wonderful time."

"You, too." I ran my fingers through my hair and headed to the pool area. I wasn't wearing a swimsuit, and it wasn't required, so I didn't know what we'd be doing at the pool. I entered through the women's change room. Courtney was standing inside looking at a tablet. As she greeted me, I remembered seeing her fiancée Dario at Lakeview Inn. Maybe I should casually bring that up. Or maybe not. I'd have to invent a reason for why I'd visited the competition.

"Hi, Courtney. How goes the great matchmaking adventure?"

She gave me a bit of a tight smile, so I guessed it might not be going well. "Hello, Quinn. You'll find a robe on the chair there. You and..." She hesitated and looked down at her tablet. "You and your date will get pedicures and reflexology treatments today, so you can get ready and go out onto the pool deck. You'll find the foot baths out there. Have fun." She shook her head at the tablet and walked away before I could respond.

"Okay, thanks," I said to the empty space, but I was too excited for a foot treatment to care. It had been a while. I wouldn't mind if Bernardo was an ogre. I was going to enjoy this.

I changed into the robe and went out onto the pool deck. Two bubbling foot baths sat facing the windows. A woman gave me a warm, fragrant towel to wrap around my neck and gestured for me to take a seat at one of the baths. "Soak your feet, and we'll be with you in a moment," she said.

"Thank you."

The healing aroma of eucalyptus rose from the bath. Large picture windows gave a spectacular view of the cove, and with the sun streaming in, this was going to be heaven. I slipped my feet into the warm, sudsy water. *Oh, bliss.* Why didn't I soak my feet more often? Leaning back, I let out a long breath and felt the tension release from my body.

On the table next to me was a bouquet of sunflowers. I loved how the giant yellow flower heads made me think of long summer days. Leaning closer, I touched one.

My fingers went right through the flower, startling me. *Holy cow!* I touched another. And another. The flowers weren't there. It was happening again! Was I delusional? I squeezed my eyes shut.

Behind me, I heard the massage therapist give the same instructions to someone else. Bernardo, I presumed. *Oh no.* Had either of them seen me reaching for imaginary sunflowers? What if I did something like that again? I didn't want to make a fool of myself. My stomach turned over as I tried to plaster on a smile to greet Bernardo. I didn't recognize him. He was good-looking, possibly South American or Mediterranean, and probably had to shave twice a day to keep his dark five o'clock shadow at bay.

He wasn't smiling. He was looking at me funny, then his gaze hit the table where my delusional bouquet sat, except I was positive he wasn't seeing it.

"What were you just doing?" he asked. "It looked like you were reaching for something."

There wasn't enough oxygen in the room. *Don't hyperventilate.* "Nothing. I—I—I thought I saw a spider hanging by a thread."

He narrowed his gaze and tossed his scented towel onto the chair beside me but didn't make a move to sit down. If he'd caught wind of the gossip about me, he could think it was true. I was cuckoo.

Spots danced in front of my eyes. Were they real? Was I having a panic attack? *I can't go on a date if I don't know what I can touch and what I can't.*

I stood, bracing myself with one hand on the back of my chair. "I'm sorry. I'm not feeling well. I'm going to have to go back to my room."

"What? You can't go anywhere. We have a date."

I couldn't quite read his expression, but it wasn't consideration. He almost looked hostile. *Why is he looking at me like that?* My fingers went numb.

I let go of the chair. "Sorry, Bernardo, but I won't be good company." I took a step toward the door.

He grabbed my arm and lowered his voice. "You're sticking your nose into things that are none of your business. So back off. Now. We're watching you, Quinn Delaney." He let me go and left the pool area from the way he'd come.

Chapter Fifteen

Too discombobulated for words, I stood with my mouth open, watching Bernardo leave the pool area. *He threatened me.*

"Hello there, I'm Louise," came from behind.

I turned and saw two women in white coats. Hopefully, they weren't here to take me away to a padded room. "We'll be doing your reflexology treatments today." She looked around. "What happened to the gentleman?"

"Something suddenly came up. He had to leave."

"Okay," she intoned. "Do you still want your treatment?"

The word no almost escaped my lips, but then I realized this could be just what I needed to calm my nerves and help me feel grounded.

By the time the reflexology treatment ended, and my toenails boasted a warm brown polish—earth tones were in—I was not only feeling better, I felt empowered. *Screw Bernardo.* I'd never been a person who backed down from a challenge, especially at this age. Reaching fifty had made me more self-assured and less a people-pleaser, not to mentioned I'd faced a few murderers now and come out on top.

If Bernardo thought I was going to stop poking around, he'd underestimated this menopausal woman. I wasn't going to let him tell me what to do. His threat only served to add him to my suspect list, and as soon as my polish dried, I was going to contact Nell and find out who Bernardo was, how he knew I was poking around, and why he cared.

After tipping the therapist, I changed into my clothes and left the pool area. I sent Nell a text telling her I had something important to discuss. As I was putting my phone away, I saw Courtney and Dario in conversation down the hall. Courtney looked excited and was squealing about something. As I approached, I heard her say, "I can't believe he's buying us a house! I love your uncle."

She was beaming as I approached. "I'm so excited! I didn't realize family doctors made so much money in Columbia."

Dario's back was facing me, but I heard him say, "He's got other stuff going on. Nothing's free, you know, everything comes with a price. He'll expect—"

"Hey, Quinn," Courtney interrupted Dario when she realized I wanted to speak to her. "You're finished with your date already? How did it go?"

I hesitated. Should I tell Courtney about Bernardo's threat? *No.* I'd have to explain what business he thought I was poking my nose into or play dumb about that. *Should I make something up?* Lying didn't come easy to me, and I'd rather avoid bumbling my words. Since Courtney didn't know I was investigating Alicia's death, I shouldn't say anything until I talked to Nell. "Well, the treatment was fantastic. My feet feel ten years younger, but the date didn't turn out well at all. He didn't stay for the treatment."

She looked confused. "He didn't stay? Why not?"

"I guess I'm not his type," I said.

"Hey." Dario nudged Courtney's arm. "Gotta interrupt here because I'm heading over to the doc's to get them back online." So, Dario did work with other clients. That could explain what he was doing at Lakeview yesterday.

He turned to me. His gaze seemed intense for some reason. "Hope things work out better next time."

When he walked away, I turned my attention back to Courtney. There was a question she could clear up. "Frankly, I'm puzzled by how we ended up in a match in the first place. We didn't speak to each other at the mixer, so we didn't choose each other as potential dates. Was he matched with me based on his profile? I've known Nell a long time. I think she'd have a good idea who to match me with."

Courtney rolled her top lip. "Maybe, but if I remember correctly, your profile was not our usual standard." Her tone was judgmental, although I couldn't blame her for that.

"Right. I apologize for that. We'd had a few drinks and were being silly. Immature. We didn't intend for those forms to be handed in, which is another puzzle to be solved."

"I don't know how puzzling it is. Melody gave them to me. She said she found them on her desk."

Melody? I didn't say anything, but Melody was definitely up to no good.

"Anyway, it's okay, Courtney," I said. My phone rang, so I excused myself and took Nell's call.

"Do you have a few minutes to talk?" I asked her as I walked away.

"Yes, but not long. Quinn, I've got a major situation here. I just found out Alicia was going to fire Melody, and now I've got to figure out if I can get through this competition without her."

"Alicia was going to fire her for poaching the competition's clients?"

"It was worse than that. Alicia learned Melody was giving other event planners lousy reviews. She was trying to discredit her competition by complaining about them getting quantities wrong, being disorganized, and about hidden costs. Alicia intended to lodge a complaint with the Event Planner's Association to get Melody's certification removed."

"Well, that's pretty serious. If Alicia threatened Melody's livelihood, that seems like a motive for murder." I'd lowered my voice.

"I know. It's disturbing to think about. I'm scrambling to see if I can replace her, but at this late date, it could mean disaster for the competition and everything we've worked so hard for."

"Why didn't Alicia tell you about this?" I asked.

"I don't know. I imagine she intended to, but Alicia couldn't stand to make a mistake, and since she was the one who hired Melody, I bet she was trying to find a replacement before telling me about it. That way, she could say she had everything under control."

That makes sense, considering Alicia's personality. "If you suspect Melody had something to do with Alicia's death, perhaps you should get the police involved."

"Maybe, but I don't know. I'm up to my eyeballs right now. I don't have one second to spare. Winning this contest means everything to me." I could hear the strain and the hope in her voice. She was struggling with what losing her event planner could mean to her chance of winning.

"Sorry, Nell, but I've got more bad news." I told her about Bernardo and his threat. "Do you have any idea how he'd be aware I was poking around? Or who he meant by we? Do you know if he knew Alicia?"

"No, I don't. I can't even picture him at the moment. I'll look into it." She sounded even more harried. "I can't stand the thought of putting you in danger, Quinn."

I understood, but this wasn't my first investigation, and I had Toni and Brielle on my side as well as an irrepressible hunger to get to the truth. And besides that, I was dreaming about Alicia's death every night. I was holding onto the hope that the dreams would end when we'd caught Alicia's killer. "I'll be careful. Toni and I will look into Bernardo and see if we can find a connection between him and Melody. If you can get me Bernardo's profile, then maybe we can figure out something from there."

She hesitated. "Okay. Just...I'll get it to you as soon as I can, okay?"

"Sure. One thing at a time." I hung up and spent a few minutes wondering what to do next. I meant what I said about being careful, so I intended to talk to Toni before moving forward.

I had a couple of hours to kill before she finished her date, but that wasn't enough time for a round trip to Break Thyme, and I wasn't sure I had the concentration for it. I needed to organize my thoughts. A good way to accomplish that was to get some exercise. Since I didn't often have the opportunity to swim, I changed into my bathing suit and did some laps.

"Aren't you happy I waited for you to be alone, so no one would see you talking to yourself?" Moe said when I came out of my bedroom later. Startled, my hand flew to my chest. At least I was showered and dressed.

"You're a gem, Moe," I said. Since sudden ghostly intrusions weren't unusual to me, I quickly recovered. "Thank you for trying to preserve my reputation. I'm afraid it's hanging by a thread at the moment."

Moe's expression turned sympathetic. "I know, pumpkin. Some of these folks are talking about you, and it's not favorable. I'm sure you're doing your best, but we're going to have to work harder to find you a love match."

"Speaking of that, you didn't pop into our room and take the profiles Toni and I filled in, did you?"

"Of course I did, and you're welcome. You were guaranteed failure otherwise. Everyone else handed in their forms ages ago. So, tell me all about the men you're meeting."

I let my breath out slowly to keep my exasperation under control. "That's not important, Moe. I'm trying to figure out who murdered Alicia, remember? Did you find her on the other side?"

"Yes, she's here. That's why I came to tell you there may be truth in your suspicions. Alicia is receiving an extra dose of love. That happens when a soul is traumatized while departing the earthly plane, but I stand by what I said, I won't ask her to relive that experience."

"Leave it all behind, huh?"

"Yes, literally."

"Well, that doesn't help me here in the land of the living, other than to confirm what we were already thinking."

"What can I do to brighten your day?"

Always a clown. "Did you have anything to do with the sprinklers going off in the dining room at Lakeview Inn yesterday?"

He laughed. "Do you mean the event being run by Alicia's nemesis, Becca Brister?"

"Yes."

"I do love sprinklers, but nope. That wasn't me."

So far he'd owned up to every antic, so I believed him. "Okay, then I have a favor to ask." I told him about Bernardo's threat. "Maybe you could snoop around and find out who Bernardo is and what he's hiding?"

"Have you considered the gossip was started to discredit you?" he asked, changing topics.

I remembered the brick house guy pointing at me the other night. "I guess it's possible, but I think the gossiper is someone different, not Bernardo. I didn't recognize Bernardo from the event."

Moe tapped his chin. "Hmm, I know what to do. I'll fill both their beds with pudding."

That made me laugh. "Although I do like that idea, I don't think it will be helpful. There's also Melody Pennycook to consider." I told him what I knew about Melody, although I was also losing faith that Moe would be of any help.

He appeared to be deep in thought. "She's not been nice, has she?" he said. "I know exactly what to do about her. I'll stuff her favorite cookies with toothpaste. How about that?"

I gave him a look. "You think that will help us figure out if she killed Alicia?"

His eyes lit up, as much as they could for a ghost, as if he'd just had a great idea.

"What?" I asked.

"I just remembered something about Alicia that's going to make all the difference." He glided behind me and then swooped around in front of me. "You and Alicia are the same size. She had an eye for fashion and her wardrobe is still hanging in her closet." He looked me up and down. "She had a turkey-red blazer that would complement your hair color. Yes! And the perfect dress for your figure. A teal—"

"Seriously? Stop. I'm not stealing Alicia's clothes. If you have nothing to offer beyond fashion advice, we have nothing to discuss."

Moe's eyes grew rounder as he fixed on something behind me.

"Hello!" Brielle said. "This is quite cheery. I believe your clown friend can see me, Quinn. How refreshing."

"He's dead," I said.

"Oh, dear," she said. "What a shame."

Moe looked from me to Brielle and back again. "Well, this is a surprise. Who do we have here?"

I explained my parallel-life twin to my clown-ghost acquaintance. Surprisingly, it gave me an odd sense of normalcy to have the two of them acknowledge and accept each other. Ghosts never thought I was off my rocker.

"What are you doing here again, Brielle? You can't be having another nap?"

She looked confused for a moment. "Julien and I are spending the whole day in bed. I guess I nodded off again."

Moe clapped his hands. "Did you hear that, Quinn? Now, that's the way to live. What can we do to turn the tables for you?"

"I'm fine with the tables as they are, thank you very much," I said, but that didn't stop Brielle from telling Moe all about Alec.

"You didn't mention this love interest," Moe reprimanded. "I don't think it's a good idea to put all your eggs in one basket. What do you think, Brielle?"

"I hear what you're saying, Moe, but Alec has special qualities that complement Quinn. He's even been thinking about a holiday in France. Quinn would love that!"

"Oh, I do like that," he said. "People who like to travel are curious folks and observant, too. I see why you think he would be good for Quinn—she's a curious crumpet. Tell me more about her."

"Excuse me," I said. "I'm right here, and I can run my own love life."

Moe looked down at me. "Many people think they're just fine on their own, but I learned from Alicia that being in a healthy, loving relationship has many benefits, such as living a longer life. Did you know that?"

"Really?" Brielle said. "Isn't that interesting? I can see why. Look at me. I've been getting more exercise since I met Julien."

"Outside the bedroom?" I asked, poking a little fun.

She blushed a little. "Yes, Quinn. We do leave the villa. We've been bicycling a lot. I want to keep up with him."

Alec was an avid hiker and now that I thought about it, I'd started walking more after we met. I'd wanted to be in better shape. "Okay, people, let's move on from my love life and focus on our suspects, one of whom may have threatened my longevity. I'd like to get to the bottom of that, if you don't mind, and both of you could help."

"Threatened you?" Brielle said. "Why didn't you say so? What do you want me to do?"

Chapter Sixteen

I WAS IN OUR cabin when Toni returned from her date.

"My horse had asthma," she said, rubbing the back of her neck. "I've never seen a horse sneeze so much, the poor thing. It was so skittish, it nearly bucked me off when a squirrel crossed our path, and it tried to bite me twice."

"That sounds even worse than my date," I confessed. I told her about Bernardo's threat.

Her eyes grew wide. "The thug. How dare he! Well, we're not running away with our tails between our legs. Are we?"

"No, we're not. He said we're watching. So, he's working with somebody."

Toni nodded, slowly. "Right. But how do they know we're looking into Alicia's murder?"

I wish I knew. "That's something we have to figure out."

"Hmm. I wonder if I ended up with that troublesome horse on purpose. When we returned to the stables, one of the stable boys said they don't usually send Horace the horse out on trail rides, not after he threw a woman, and she broke her hip."

"Oh, Toni. You could have been hurt. So, how did you end up with that horse?"

She threw up her hands. "I don't know. I'd like to think it was an honest mistake."

I agreed but still had a bad feeling about it. "It's hard to swallow that someone would try to do us harm, but I still want to know who scheduled you with Horace."

"Considering how suspicious Melody is looking, and since she's the event coordinator, it could have been her, but she would have had to have been sneaky about it. She wouldn't have any authority over the horses. Should we talk to Nell about all this?"

Maybe it was Melody, but it could also be Bernardo. Or the other someone he referred to. "Nell's having a horrible day and has enough to deal with at the moment. Let's go talk to the stable people and see if they can tell us who put you with Horace."

As we walked to the stables, I asked Toni if there were any potential sparks between her and Clark.

"Not so far, but mostly because I was concentrating so hard on the horse. I don't even remember what we talked about."

"Are you going on another date with him?"

"Yes, indeed," she said. "He felt badly when he realized what a hard time I'd had with Horace, so we're going to have dinner tonight. You don't mind, do you?"

It thrilled me to see Toni embracing this experience. "No, of course not. I'll go into Break Thyme while you're on your hot date. Are you looking forward to it?"

"I am. This event is proving more enlightening than I'd imagined. I didn't think I'd be learning new things about myself at this stage in life, but I am."

I thought about that for a second and realized how important it was to take risks, put ourselves out there and have new experiences or we might stop learning about ourselves. Maybe that was a reason to take this dating seriously. "That's a good thing, my friend. What have you learned?"

She waggled her eyebrows. "I'm actually more charming than I thought. At least two men have told me so. And, I always figured, if I ever dated again, I'd go for a man just like Norman, you know, an academic with a good sense of humor, who's self-controlled, patient, forgiving and a family man."

Norman had been all those things and more. The only negative comment Toni had ever voiced of her husband was when she'd thought he was too darn nice, and people took advantage of him. "I don't see anything wrong with that. Those are all admirable qualities. Are you saying you want something else in a man?"

We crossed the road and followed the path to the stables. I zipped my coat against the sudden wind.

"Both Clark and Lennox are more gregarious than Norman was. It's been an eye opener to be around men like that. It surprised me to find them energizing since I'm more of an introvert."

"That's interesting. You don't shy away from people, though. You seem comfortable in a crowd."

"Well, if I had to choose between staying home with a good book or going out with a group of people, I'd take the book every time."

"Hmm, I'd probably choose the people over the book, although I do like to read at bedtime."

"You've always been more social than me," Toni said. "That's why you're up front at Break Thyme and I'm in the kitchen baking. Our differences seem to work for us since we've been pretty good friends for thirty-two years."

"The best," I said as we reached the stable.

Inside, the earthy smell of hay and horses greeted us. We followed the sound of clinking metal bits to find a young woman with long blonde braids removing the bridle from a horse.

"Excuse me," I said as she looked over at us. "We're wondering who to talk to about the scheduling of the trail rides. I mean, who decides what horse to put with the guests?"

"Bonnie does that," she said. "But she's off for the rest of the day. Can I help you with something?" A whinny and stamping sound came from one stall.

"Yes," Toni said, glancing toward the stalls. "We're with the Heart to Heart group. I just finished a trail ride on Horace."

The woman's gaze narrowed. "We don't usually send old Horace out on trail rides with guests."

"Well, I wish that was the case, but he did today," Toni said. "I'm not complaining. We'd just like to know who gave the okay for Horace to go out if that's not the usual practice."

"I don't know. If you want, I can ask around."

"Yes, please. That would be great," Toni said.

"We'll wait here," I suggested.

She brushed her hands off on her pants. "Okay. I'll be right back."

Toni scrolled through her photos. "I can show them a picture of Melody and ask if they saw her here this morning. She posed with a bunch of us."

It wasn't long before the woman returned with a guy who sauntered toward us, his hands shoved into the front pockets of his jeans.

"You wanted to know who gave the okay for Horace to go out on the trail today," the guy said.

"Yes. I'm wondering if it was this woman?" Toni asked, holding her phone for him to see.

He didn't look at the phone. "I don't know who made the change. We go from the schedule that gets print-ed out every morning." He gestured toward a bulletin board on the wall. "This morning, someone crossed out Daisy's name and replaced it with Horace. I'm new here. I thought the boss made the change, and the rider was experienced enough to give Horace some exercise."

Toni let go her breath and pointed to Melody in the photo. "Did either of you see this woman around the stables this morning?"

They leaned in to look.

"Nope," the guy said.

"I've seen her around the resort, but not at the stables," said the young woman.

The guy tilted Toni's phone closer to him and squinted. "That woman was at the stables this morning."

"What woman?" Toni and I asked together.

I stepped closer to see who he was pointing to.

"That's Courtney," Toni said, looking at me.

The guy stepped back. "I nearly ran into her coming out of the office. She said she was looking for Margot, but there's no one by that name working here."

Odd. Courtney was at the stables this morning, and she'd also set me up with Bernardo, who'd then threatened me. Was Courtney in cahoots with Bernardo? Why? We'd found no reason to suspect Courtney in Alicia's death. "Thank you," I said to the two young people and pulled Toni aside.

"Wait," Toni said to the woman. "Can you show us the printout where the name of the horse was changed?"

"I guess so," the pig-tailed woman said. "It's tacked to the board in the office." She waved for us to follow.

"Wonderful. Thank you very much." Toni said when she snapped a photo of the schedule.

I was eager to discuss this new turn of events. Was there a reasonable explanation for Courtney to have been at the stables this morning?

"I'd like to find a connection between Bernardo and either Courtney, Melody or Becca."

"Good idea. I was thinking it would be good to know if it was Courtney who changed the horses." Toni said.

"How are we going to do that?"

Toni waggled her phone at me. "The change to the schedule was done in writing. It may be a long shot, but maybe we can match the handwriting in the photo I took to Courtney's handwriting. We just need to get a sample of hers."

I looked at the photo and saw the word Horace scrawled above the name Daisy, which was scratched out. The handwriting was small, with the letters printed close together. Not the most legible script.

"Good thinking, but how will we get a sample of Courtney's handwriting? Who writes anything by hand these days?"

"We'll ask her to write something for us," Toni suggested. "We can say Nell needs it."

"Okay, it's worth a try, unless she purposely disguised her handwriting."

"I guess that's a possibility. Let's go to the main lodge and see if we can find her."

The door to the Heart to Heart office was open. Courtney sat at a desk working on her computer. I rapped my knuckles against the door to get her attention. She stopped typing and looked up.

"Hi, Courtney. We just ran into Nell and a couple of guests who wanted to know about the vegetarian options for the meals tomorrow. Nell asked if you could write them down. With the latest shenanigans, she wants to be sure everything is in order. We offered to deliver the information to the guests since Nell is pretty busy."

"Really?" She twisted her mouth, thinking. "The resort would have that information."

"Nell sounded like she wanted to be as helpful as possible," said Toni. "Do you not have the menu?"

Courtney looked down at her computer screen and clicked on a folder. "Yes, I have it. Just a sec."

As she searched, I grabbed a notebook from my purse and placed it on the desk, smack dab in front of her. Off to the side of her keyboard sat a notepad. Written on top was the name of a florist with a phone number. The script was feminine looking, with loops and swirls. Courtney was planning a wedding, so this could be her note. If she'd written this, then her handwriting was not at all similar to whoever wrote the word Horace on the horse-riding schedule.

Behind her, the printer whirled into action. Oh shoot, she was printing the menu instead of writing the vegetarian dishes like I'd asked. "You don't have to print the entire menu. Can you just write the vegetarian options?" I nudged the notepad closer to her right hand.

"This is easier than writing them out." Courtney spun her chair around and snatched a couple of sheets from the printer. "Here you go."

"Which ones are vegetarian?"

"The ones with the asterisks beside them."

"Would you mind jotting down *vegetarian* beside the asterisk, so the guests will know?" I'd better remember to tell Nell we'd asked Courtney to do this.

She let go an impatient breath, but thankfully picked up the pen and wrote vegetarian. Toni peered over my shoulder and frowned. Based on Courtney's handwriting, it was very unlikely she'd been the one to change the horse's name. Maybe she really had been looking for someone named Margot at the stables this morning. Perhaps a guest.

I picked up the menu. "Thanks, Courtney. Appreciate it."

"You must be getting excited about your wedding," Toni said. "When's the big day?"

Courtney's face brightened. "Seven weeks and four days. And it's not just the wedding I'm planning. We've decided to move to Columbia. If we do that, then we can afford to try for a baby right away. When Dario joins his uncle's business, I'll never have to work again."

"What business is that?" I asked.

"He's a doctor, but he has an ongoing project for Dario. I'm not exactly sure of all the details. Something to do with tech."

"A techy doctor?" I asked. "My doctor isn't tech savvy at all."

Courtney shrugged.

"Well, that all sounds very exciting," Toni said. "Best of luck, Courtney, and thank you again. We'll let you get back to work."

In the lobby, Toni said, "So, unless she was savvy enough to disguise her handwriting, Courtney was not responsible for Horace the horrid horse. At least not in any way we can prove at this point."

I was relieved to scratch Courtney off the suspect list and not because she had no motive for killing Alicia, at least not that we'd uncovered, but because she had an exciting new life planned. I was happy for her. "I agree. After what Nell said about Alicia's plans to fire Melody, I think she's our most likely suspect. We need to find out if she has an alibi for Sunday night."

Toni looked at her watch. "I'm sorry, Quinn. I have to meet Clark for an early dinner, and I've got a few things I'd like to do first. Can this wait?"

"Sure. Have a great time, and I'll see you later."

I was suddenly eager to get over to Break Thyme. An urgent feeling rose in me, as if I needed to hurry. Thoughts of Adelaide popped into my head. I might have dismissed the thought as a random occurrence, but I was starting to believe there was purpose in these experiences.

I grabbed my phone, found Adelaide's contact information, and sent her a text. *Hi Adelaide. Quinn here. We met at the psychic fair. I'll be in Bookend Bay this afternoon. Would like to connect. Let me know if this works for you?*

Chapter Seventeen

By the time I reached the parking lot in Moose Harbor, I had no message from Adelaide, so I looked at the boats docked in the harbor on the chance I'd see her. This might have been easier if I'd asked the name of her boat. *Some investigator you are.* At least I remembered she inherited a sailboat, so I only needed to look for boats with masts.

As I wandered along the dock, it amazed me there were so many boats parked in slips at the Moose Harbor Yacht Club. *Why were so few people out sailing?* Maybe because there was no wind, at least not at that moment, but the harbor was always filled with boats. Out in the bay, at least a dozen sailboats bobbed in the calm water. If Adelaide's boat was one of those, I wouldn't find her here.

A woman scrubbing her deck nodded to me and said hello as I passed. The hatch was open on the next sailboat, so I paused long enough to peer inside, although I only saw a counter and bench seating.

Brielle and Julien would sail the Mediterranean together. After living in Longfellow last summer, I could easily see myself living in small quarters. I'd loved having so little to look after. It had been freeing in ways I couldn't have imagined.

"Hey, Quinn," Harvey called from his deck, waving at me with what looked like a wrench in his hand. He was a regular at Break Thyme. "What brings you onto the dock?"

"I'm looking for a friend, a woman. Long, white hair. Her name is Adelaide. She has a sailboat somewhere in the harbor. You haven't seen someone like that, have you?"

He shook his head. "Nope. Haven't seen anyone like that around the club either."

"Okay, thanks anyway."

"Sure. Good luck!"

Coming up empty-handed, I couldn't help feeling disappointed as I reached Break Thyme. I'd really thought I was meant to run into Adelaide.

While it was comforting to have Toni to talk to about my paranormal experiences, I didn't know anyone besides Brielle who was having similar episodes. It would be nice to have someone who understood what it was like to live in a world where weird things happened. I'd just had a feeling Adelaide and I would relate to each other. But maybe I was so desperate not to be alone in this that I'd read more into meeting her than I should have.

My phone dinged. I stopped to read a text from Alec. *Hey you, how's the murder-date going? Hope you're staying safe. I'm making a seafood chowder for our date. You don't have any allergies, do you? I've been thinking about you a lot. Can't wait to see you.*

Warmth filled me as I read the last two lines of his message. His tone had definitely changed lately. Maybe the thought of me at a dating event had something to do with that. I was looking forward to seeing him too, so I told him so and assured him I had no food allergies.

I was smiling when I entered Break Thyme through the kitchen. Since I hadn't had lunch, my stomach growled as I hung my coat in the closet, tucked away my purse, donned an apron, washed my hands, and stepped into the café. I took a moment to survey the room. Things often slowed down later in the day.

"There you are," said Poppy when she spied me behind the counter.

"Hey, Poppy, how have things been?"

"Good. About the usual, as far as customers go." She placed her handful of dishes on the counter.

I glanced at the scones under glass. Pastries were not a healthy lunch, so I had to be strong and resist. I had salad ingredients in the fridge.

"A woman asked about you," Poppy said. "She didn't say her name, but she might still be in the Nook."

I thought of Adelaide, of course, but then why would she not have answered my text? "Okay, thanks." I put my hunger on the back burner and checked out the Nook, seeing her right away. Her striking silver hair made her easy to spot. She looked like she was getting ready to leave. She'd put on her coat.

"Hi, Adelaide," I said, joining her at the table. "It's great to see you again. We must be on the same wavelength because I sent you a text about an hour ago asking if you wanted to meet."

"You did? I'm sorry about not getting back to you. I had an accident with my phone and need to get a replacement."

"Oh, dear. Phone accidents can send life into a turmoil."

"Yes, I guess that's true, but if truth be told, I just got a cell phone a few months ago and sometimes I feel like I was better off without one."

Holy cow. How did anyone manage these days without a cell phone?

"I know," she said, reading my thoughts. "It always shocks people to hear that. I'm a true dinosaur. I would have been quite happy to have been born a couple of centuries ago. Anyway, I'm glad I caught you. I was hoping to talk to you again. I may be new to the world of psychic fairs, but I do believe things happen for a reason—as in our paths crossing."

"Me, too, and ours have crossed twice. I wanted to ask you about the conversation we had with Kya. Did any of it make sense to you? Were you able to talk to her about it further?"

"No. She mentioned faeries, witches, and magic. I do not mess with that stuff. I've had some uncomfortable experiences and intend to keep my energy positive. I've changed everything about my life because the way things were going...well, I'll just say, everything depends upon nurturing myself right now and building a stress-free life.

I could relate. I was also reluctant to mess with that stuff. Who knew what I might inadvertently invite into my life? It sounded like Adelaide hadn't had it easy. "I understand. I've also been through some major life changes. A divorce. New business. Getting to know myself better and paying closer attention to my intuition."

She smiled and nodded. "Sounds familiar. I'm also starting my own business."

"Congratulations. I love working for myself. It's scary and exhausting, but so rewarding. I wouldn't want to be doing anything else."

She looked around the café, her gaze pausing for a second on the picture windows that faced Courtesy Park and Lake Superior making the Cozy Nook feel like it was part of the outdoors. My bevy of potted plants enhanced the effect.

"You've done a beautiful job with your café. People must love coming here." She touched a lavender plant in the center of the table. "I especially like your herbal theme."

"Thank you. So, what business are you starting?"

"I'm opening a small shop that sells all natural products—essential oils, herbal remedies, skin care—those kinds of things. I've been doing it for years for myself and friends. They raved about my healing products, calling them miracle cures. When I got to the point where I couldn't keep up, I realized I have a viable business."

I'd had similar positive feedback from my friends about my artisan drinks. "That sounds perfect. So when did things get weird?"

"It was just...uh." She hesitated and her face flushed pink. "People started having adverse reactions and stopped buying my products. The town I live in has more than its fair share of superstitions. I'm concerned I could be ostracized. I don't know what I'll do if my business doesn't survive."

By the strain in her eyes, I could tell this was causing her grief and wished I could help. I wasn't sure what superstition had to do with her credibility, but I didn't feel comfortable pushing for details since we hardly knew each other.

"Do you have someone who can help you understand the adverse reactions?" She must have considered the ingredients in her products. Maybe something was off.

She let out a weary breath and shook her head. "I don't know. I...I've always believed in the power of positive thinking, and that you manifest what you truly believe." She hesitated, gave me a piercing look as if I was supposed to read between the lines, and then appeared to redirect her thoughts. "After what Kya said about my powers being a mess, I'm worried about my ability to keep my thoughts positive. I can't let my business fail. Not after everything I've been through."

I understood why her business was important to her, but I didn't know why she thought she could fix this with positive thinking. Maybe she wasn't telling me the complete story. "For as long as you're here in Bookend Bay, I can be a sounding board if you need someone to talk to."

"I appreciate that." She opened her mouth as if to continue but looked around the room first. Then she spoke in a lowered voice. "I hope you won't think I'm daft, but the last time we met, I had a...reaction, and I can't get it out of my head. Sometimes things come to me about other people. It's why my healing remedies have been so successful. Can I share something with you?"

"Yes, and please don't worry about what I'll think. I've had some pretty bizarre experiences myself." I didn't want to get into the murder I was trying to solve, but I wanted to share something to make her comfortable. "For instance, when we first met, I saw a bottle of broken walnut oil on the floor between us. You didn't happen to see that, did you?"

"No, I didn't. I wasn't sure what you were talking about. But I'll tell you this. I believe the things you're seeing are good for you. You're manifesting what you need in your life, and you're seeing these things because you're second-guessing something important. You need to trust yourself."

I need oils and sunflowers in my life? "I'm not sure I understand."

"I'm sorry. I don't know specifics, but I do believe you'll understand. Soon."

Something about Adelaide, her energy, I suppose, made me feel better about my weird life.

"I hope I've eased your worries some, Quinn. I'd like to chat longer, but I've got so much to do. I've got to get my sailboat up for sale, or I'll be stuck paying another month's docking fees. It's expensive!" She picked up her purse, a white clutch printed with small blue anchors, and set it on her knee. I wondered if she bought the purse before she inherited a sailboat. "And you have a business to run, so I'll let you get to it. I'd love to talk again another time."

"I'd like that." I had the feeling we both had secrets we were reluctant to share, especially in a public place. We said goodbye.

I got to work. Luckily, the tasks I needed to accomplish were routine and didn't require too many brain cells because Adelaide's message had me distracted. I wanted to believe my manifestations were good for me. It helped that I'd felt an unexplained kinship with Adelaide, but I still had another puzzle to solve.

For the rest of the afternoon, I focused on work, and it was a good thing I'd done so because just as I finished placing our weekly order, Brielle popped in. She looked around, orienting herself. It must be strange to not know where you'd materialized until you arrived.

"We need to talk about Bernardo," she said. "He's not who he says he is."

Chapter Eighteen

As soon as we were upstairs with the door closed, Brielle started talking. "I poked around in the Heart to Heart client files."

"How did you get into their system?" I asked.

She gave a cocky smile. "Easy. I just watched Courtney log in and got the password. I thought it would be harder, but she's a slow typist."

Invisibility was a great asset. I marveled at Brielle's ability to behave like a fly on the wall, but I didn't covet the skill. Other than to catch a killer, I didn't want inside information on anyone in my life or inadvertently learn what people said about me. To me, this ability worked best in a world where no one knew you existed, like in Brielle's case.

"So, what did you learn?" I asked her.

"For one, there's no one named Bernardo at this event."

I thought back to the message I'd received. "I got a text message saying my date was with Bernardo. The message came from Heart to Heart. I checked. I was told to meet him in the pool area, and Courtney greeted me there."

"Does Courtney have a motive to have wanted Alicia out of the picture?"

"Not that we know of. But someone at Heart to Heart set me up with Bernardo."

"Did you tell Nell about Bernardo's threat?"

"I did, but I don't think his name registered with her. She was in the middle of the Melody crisis." I updated her on that. "Alicia intended to discredit Melody officially, which could have destroyed her budding business."

"Sounds like a motive for murder, no?"

"I agree and said as much to Nell. But we don't understand how Bernardo fits in. Unless he's a hired thug."

I wished Toni was here to discuss this. A glance at my watch showed it was nearly six o'clock. She must be on her dinner date with Clark. "We need to look for a connection between Bernardo and Melody, and then we'll have something solid to take to the police."

Brielle opened her mouth to say something and then poof! She disappeared, leaving me staring at my Ficus tree.

I was back at Great Bear Lodge lying in my bed texting with Alec. *Hate to end this,* he wrote. *Early start tomorrow, so gotta get shut eye. Hug coming your way. Looking forward to hugging you in person.*

A hug sounded pretty nice. I told him so, then we said goodnight. I yawned and stretched, thankful I was already in pajamas with my face washed and teeth brushed.

It was quarter after ten. Where was Toni? She must be having a great time to be out so late. I got out of bed and looked out the front window. Gosh, it was dark. I guess I'd gotten used to living on Courtesy Boulevard where streetlights shone through the night. I stood there for a few minutes, watching blackened trees swaying in the wind.

My legs were crampy, and my back wasn't feeling all that hot either. The latest Rhys Bowen novel was waiting for me on my bedside table. I could read while waiting for Toni.

I woke with a start. That darn dream again had my heart pounding. I must have fallen asleep while reading. Light shining from my bedside lamp had me squinting until my eyes adjusted. My watch read two-twelve. I got out of bed and went to the bathroom.

On my way back to my bedroom, I noticed Toni's door was open. She usually closed her door. Surely, she'd come home by now. I quietly peered inside. In the dark, it was hard to see, so I stepped closer to the bed. She wasn't there!

I flicked on the lights and checked the other side of the bed, just in case she'd slipped and fallen, but no Toni. *Oh my gosh, where is she?*

I scrambled back to my room and checked my phone to see if she'd sent a text. It didn't matter how magical her date was, she'd never stay out until two in the morning without letting me know.

Someone switched Toni's horse. Bernardo threatened me. What if he did something to Toni?

Get dressed. Find help!

Where are my socks? I don't need socks. A bra? Yes, a bra. Where is it? Forget the bra.

I snatched my jacket off the hook by the door, stuffed my feet into shoes, grabbed my phone, and ran down the road to the lobby. She'd been with Clark. *I must talk to Clark. A staff member must be available in case of an emergency. They have his number. They can call Clark.*

My foot caught on something on the path. I tripped and nearly fell face first onto the gravel road. A big help I'd be if I broke a bone.

You're panicking. Slow down.

Lighting was minimal, so I found the flashlight on my phone and carried on while watching my step.

In the lobby, I hurried to the front desk and rang the bell. A few seconds later, a freckle-faced young man came out of an office. His name tag said Jason. "Can I help you?" he asked.

"Yes, please. My friend is missing. She didn't come back to our room after her date. We're with the Heart to Heart people."

"Okay. So, she's not answering her phone?"

I looked at the phone in my hand. I'd checked for a text from Toni, but I hadn't called her. "Um. I'm sorry. I panicked." I hit the call button. Jason and I stared at my phone while it rang. On the fourth ring, it connected.

"Hello," came Toni's groggy voice.

"Toni! Where are you? Are you okay?"

"Uh..." she hesitated. I heard rustling like she'd changed position. "Good grief," she said in a hushed voice. "I must have fallen asleep in Clark's room. He covered me up on the couch."

"Oh, thank God." Relief washed over me. "She's okay," I said to Jason. "I'm sorry to have bothered you."

"No bother at all. Is there anything else I can do for you?"

"No. No. Thank you very much." I stepped away toward the fireplace. "Where is Clark's room?" I asked Toni.

"I'm leaving now. It's in the lodge. I'll be in our cabin in a few minutes."

"Toni, I'm in the lobby. I'll wait for you." My heart was returning to its usual pace.

A couple of minutes later, the elevator door opened, and Toni walked out. "I can't believe I fell asleep," she said. Her hair was pushed up on one side, and she had a smudge of mascara under her left eye. "I'm sorry for worrying you."

I gave her a hug. "It's fine. That's what friends do."

"Sure. That's what friends do in normal circumstances," she said, pushing the door open. "But after what Bernardo said, you had every reason to worry."

"I could have saved myself some trouble if I'd thought to call you first instead of running off half-cocked." My reaction worried me. I'd not been thinking clearly, and that wasn't good. Not when someone staying at this resort could be Alicia's killer and knew we were poking around. "And speaking of Bernardo, Brielle learned there's no

Bernardo registered in this event. We'll need to talk to Nell about it first thing in the morning. I think there's a chance Melody realized what we're up to and sent Bernardo to warn us off."

"Hmm, well, we don't scare that easy, right?"

Something rustled in the trees alongside the road. We grabbed each other's arms. "Are there bears in these woods?" Toni whispered.

A white bunny tail flashed us as its owner scampered off. I laughed. "Nope, we don't scare easily, that's for darn sure."

Toni gave a soft snort. "As long as we don't run into anything larger than Peter Cottontail."

We made it back to the cabin with a slightly bruised sense of bravado and decided to leave further discussion to the morning when we'd hopefully be better rested.

"You know I have to ask," I said as Toni and I were getting ready for breakfast. "How'd you end up in Clark's room last night?"

She waggled her eyes coquettishly and put on her lipstick.

"Oh! Toni Miller. You didn't? Did you?"

"What? Sleep with Clark?" She smiled as if she'd been thinking about just that. "No. We hardly know each other. But that's not to say there wasn't kissing."

I swear she looked younger when she said that. "Kissing sounds pretty nice."

"It really was. I had no idea I wanted to kiss anyone, and then there I was making a move on him."

"You made the move?"

"Well, don't look so surprised."

I didn't respond to that because it wouldn't help to remind her she'd never shown a hint of interest in kissing a man. Smiling, I said, "I'm happy for you."

"Everything just felt so comfortable," she said. "I impressed him when I looked up jackalopes after he talked about them. He said I was the only person curious enough to do so. Jackalopes don't exist. They're mythical creatures. I thought it was a clever conversation starter and made him stand out."

I laughed. With everything I'd been dealing with, I'd forgotten about that. "Good for you."

"We had a lovely conversation over dinner and then we went for a walk. It was getting chilly, and we were enjoying each other's company so much, Clark invited me up to see his suite. He upgraded his room. It's lovely. We had a nightcap and put on the fire. I was getting tired and should have come home, but I didn't want to leave. He had to take a phone call, and that's the last thing I remember. I must have fallen asleep."

I guessed Clark didn't think that Toni's roommate might wake up in the middle of the night, check on her like a mother hen, and fly into a panic when she wasn't in bed. The mother hen in me had deep roots.

"I should call him and thank him for such an enjoyable night." She retrieved her phone from the counter.

"Okay. You do that, and I'll meet you at the lodge," I said, thinking she might like some privacy for her call. Since the sun was beaming, I grabbed my sunglasses from the top of the dresser in the bedroom.

"I won't be long. Meet you in the dining room," she said with the phone to her ear.

I wanted to find Nell first. She hadn't responded to my text. "Sure. I'm going to stop in at the Heart to Heart office first."

"Okay. If you're not in the dining room, I'll check the—" She pointed at her phone. "Good morning, Clark."

I gave her a thumbs up and left the room. Outside, the warm air was a nice surprise since I hadn't checked the weather forecast. I tossed my sweater back inside, then headed over to the main lodge. On the way, I called Nell but got her voicemail.

A few people were milling around in the lobby. "Looks like it's going to be a beautiful day," I said to a couple of women I recognized from the event.

Then I saw Melody and Courtney sitting on a couch by the window. *Hmm.* I wondered if Nell had talked to Melody about maligning her competition. I walked their way.

Melody was doing the talking as I approached. "I booked the transport for your wedding guests from the church to the venue. Send me the changes you want to make to the seating chart, and I'll take care of that, too," she said, standing. Melody must be Courtney's wedding planner.

"Good morning," Melody said to me cheerfully. "So much to do. Can't chat. I've got to get set up in the dining room for our breakfast meeting. See you there!" Okay, so she didn't sound like a woman who'd been confronted and fired, so Nell hadn't spoken to Melody yet. I couldn't really blame Nell, considering how much this event depended on Melody's management.

"Good morning, Courtney. Do you know where Nell is?"

"Hi, Quinn," Courtney said, standing and smoothing her skirt. "Nell is off site this morning. She had an emergency to deal with."

"Oh? I hope it's nothing serious."

"She didn't say, but I hope not, too. Things are pretty busy here."

But you still have time to talk about your wedding details. "No doubt."

"Quinn?" came a man's voice behind me.

I turned to see a man I'd spoken with at the mixer. Mac, the security guard. I remembered his occupation because I'd used mnemonics—Mac attack. "Good morning, Mac. How are you?"

"I'm fine. It's you I've been worried about."

"Why are you worried about me?"

He cocked his head as if I'd asked a strange question. "Because you didn't show up for our date yesterday."

"What date? When?" *Was I supposed to have had a dinner date with Mac?*

"Our date at Cranberry Cove Conservation Park. Yesterday morning. I received a text telling me to meet you there."

I looked at Courtney. She shook her head. "We didn't send anyone to Cranberry Cove. That's over an hour's drive, isn't it?"

"Yeah, it is," Mac said, looking perturbed. I couldn't blame him.

"Can you show me the text?" I said and pulled out my phone.

He found the message and turned his cell so I could read it. Courtney moved closer. Sure enough, the message said his date was with me and he should meet me at Cranberry Cove. The sender was Heart to Heart, just like my message.

"I sent out all the texts yesterday from the company cell phone," Courtney said. "I'm sure I didn't send that one."

"Well, someone did, someone who had access to your phone," Clark said.

Courtney ran her hand through her chestnut hair. "I don't know how that happened. I—um…" She looked at me. "I'm going to call Nell." Courtney hurried off toward the Heart to Heart office.

Whoever sent Mac that text yesterday must have accessed the company files to get his phone number. Did we have a reason to suspect Courtney?

Mac clicked his tongue and shook his head. "Who do you think didn't want us to have a date yesterday? I was happy to be paired with you."

I looked at him, shook my head, and caught sight of Toni coming in the front door. "I have no idea, and I would have preferred a date with you, too. I'm sorry. Can you please excuse me? My friend has just arrived."

"Sure, but we should talk to that Courtney gal and be sure we get our date."

Alec's playful smile popped into my head. "Okay. You can leave that to me. I'll talk to her." But now I wasn't sure I wanted to date Mac.

"Good morning," Toni said to Mac. "I'm Toni. I don't think we met."

"I'm Mac. Nice to meet you." He stepped back and looked at me. "Quinn, let me know how your talk with Courtney goes, especially if she learns anything about those messages. I'll see you later."

"Those messages?" Toni questioned.

"Yes. I was supposed to have a date with Mac yesterday, but someone sent him a text telling him to go to Cranberry Cove for our date."

"That's a bit of a drive."

"Yes, it is. And they set me up with Bernardo."

"I guess we can assume the bogus texts were to give Bernardo a chance to deliver his threat and maybe even worse," Toni said. "Because it seems like a lot of trouble to go to just to tell you to mind your own business."

She was right. "Good grief. Things could have been worse since it was me who ended our date, not him. I hallucinated the vase of sunflowers and had a panic attack."

Toni grimaced. "Because you backed out, the worst he could do was threaten you. I hate to say it, but that makes more sense."

"Those sunflowers may have saved me." A chill turned me icy cold. "Toni, I don't know where Nell is. She's not answering her phone. I think it's time to call the police."

Chapter Nineteen

"I AGREE," TONI SAID. "We should let the police know that someone threatened us, but are we going to admit we're looking into Alicia's death, or will we say we don't know what prompted Bernardo's warning?"

"You have a good point." Despite our murder-solving success rate, the police were never enthusiastic about our getting involved in an investigation, even if they weren't investigating. We'd likely get a strong reprimand and be told to heed Bernardo's "advice."

"Why don't you call Nell again?" Toni suggested. "We don't know that she's in any danger."

True. "You're right. I don't know why I'm thinking the worst. I guess because she was the one who discovered the conflict between Alicia and Melody."

Toni's eyes filled with compassion. "Quinn, you've got more than Alicia's murder to deal with. You're also having terrible dreams and hallucinations."

I took a deep breath, then let it out slowly. "When you put it that way, it sounds like I should seek professional help."

"I'd agree, but I don't think it's a good idea for you to share the details of your life with a doctor. I don't think science has caught up to you."

"No. I've got to believe the dreams will stop when we've solved Alicia's murder, and I think we're getting close. I'll try calling Nell again." Since the lobby was a busy place, we went down the hallway, where it was quieter. I dialed Nell's number and put the phone on speaker. It connected on the third ring.

"Hi, Quinn," Nell said. "Sorry I didn't get back to you. I'm just leaving the police station now."

Whew! She hadn't said she was going to the police. "Did you report the trouble between Alicia and Melody?"

"No, not exactly. This was another matter. This morning, I received a phone call from a police officer in South America. He was following up on a matter he'd discussed with Alicia just over a week ago."

"Did Alicia keep that to herself as well?"

Nell made an irritated sound. "Yes, she did. I've learned a lot about Alicia since she died. I knew she was a control freak, but I never thought she'd keep things like this from me. Mind you, this only happened the day before she died."

"What did the police want?"

"Originally, when they talked to Alicia, they'd been looking into credit card fraud."

"Credit card fraud?" Toni said. "This gets more interesting by the hour."

"Yes, it does, unfortunately," said Nell. "A few months ago, they received a rash of complaints from people about fraudulent charges on their credit cards. When they looked at the other charges on these people's credit cards, they found a common denominator—us. Everyone had also made a recent payment to Heart to Heart, so the police figured the credit card numbers were stolen by someone associated with us."

"Yikes," I said. "Do you have any idea who?"

"The only person who deals with credit card payments is Courtney."

"Well, that's interesting because the reason my date was with Bernardo, the imposter, instead of Mac was because someone from Heart to Heart sent Mac all the way to Cranberry Cove."

Nell exhaled sharply. "Courtney was responsible for sending instructions to the participants." Nell went quiet. All we heard was the sound of her car engine. "I'm trying to wrap my head around this," she finally said. "Courtney has been with us from the beginning. I can't believe she's connected to criminals who steal credit cards."

Not the first time I'd heard that note of surprise. Always shocking to learn a person you thought you knew had committed a crime. "Well, something's not right with Courtney and with Melody, too. Did you tell the police about Bernardo?"

"Oh, for goodness' sakes! Just a second. There's a family of geese on the highway."

It wasn't smart to discuss murder suspects while Nell was driving. "Nell, let's talk about this when you get back, and we'll figure out what to do next."

"Okay. I have to make a stop, so I'll see you in about forty minutes."

We said goodbye and disconnected.

Toni clicked her tongue. "Remember when we checked into the resort, the debit machine wasn't working, and the guy ahead of us offered to give Courtney his credit card information?"

"Yes, I remember that. I thought he was being too trusting."

"Me, too. It would have been obvious who stole his information if any fraudulent charges showed up, but it still seems fishy."

"Courtney complained about the debit machines being faulty," I said.

"I remember. If that has something to do with the credit card fraud, what's our next step?"

"Well, if Alicia came to the same conclusion as Nell did about Courtney stealing credit card numbers, then Alicia might have confronted Courtney and threatened to tell the police. She knew Alicia rowed every morning and could have taken her by surprise. Courtney's a heavier woman than Alicia."

"Yes, but since Alicia rowed every day, she must have had some strength to her."

"That's true, but like I said, maybe Courtney took her by surprise. Anyway, I'd like to brainstorm this with Brielle. Maybe she can use her persuasive suggestions to get Courtney to tell the truth." Last year, we'd discovered Brielle could plant suggestions in people's minds and have them act on these suggestions. This had helped us catch a killer before. I hoped it could work again.

"That's a good idea," Toni said. "Although it's early in the day for Brielle."

"Yes, unless she's spending another day in bed with Julien, drifting in and out of sleep. Unfortunately, there's no guarantee she'll show up here. She could pop in at Break Thyme. Sometimes she ends up at Beach Meadows where my trailer was. Maybe I can ask Moe to look for her."

A woman's voice shot out from the corridor that led to the washrooms. "This is not funny!"

"It nearly made me pee my pants!" came another female voice.

Two women appeared at the end of the hallway. They were holding onto each other.

"What's going on now?" Toni said as we joined them.

"Go see for yourself," the woman in a floral blazer said.

"Open the door to the ladies' room, but be prepared," said the other woman. I glanced down at her fuchsia stilettos and winced. How her feet survived in those heels was beyond me.

I walked my flat, practical shoes to the ladies' room.

"Do you want to go first?" I asked Toni.

"Chicken," she said, and pushed the door open slowly.

"Ack!" she cried and stepped back. "That's creepy."

Even though I knew to expect something, I still gasped when I saw the scarecrow. Someone positioned it to be seen when you opened the door. It had to be seven feet tall. Over-sized blue eyes with thick lashes were painted over a crooked smile on a canvas head stuffed with straw. Evidence of this poked out from under a sombrero. It wore a plaid shirt and denim overalls, but that wasn't what sent my heart into my throat—it was one of the mis-matched gloves. *Holy Hannah!*

"Toni! See that glove, the one on its right hand, the one with the orange stripe. That's the glove I saw in my dream. I'm sure of it." The glove was real! My dream hadn't been just smoke and mirrors. It had been a clear message, something I could trust. I was nearly giddy with excitement. All I had to do was to prove the scarecrow had murdered Alicia. I smiled at my own joke.

"You dreamed about this scarecrow?" The stilettoed woman asked, turning my attention.

I shook my head. "No. Not the scarecrow. Just the glove."

"Okay," the woman said, drawing out the word. "I'd hate to be in your head."

"Yes, you probably would," I said.

Toni was looking at me wide-eyed. "Where did it come from?"

I figured she meant the glove. "As far as I know, it came from the beach where…you know." The scarecrow looked suspiciously like the work of a certain prankster ghost.

"I don't get the humor in all these silly pranks," the woman in the blazer said. "I'm going to use the other washroom. That thing is creeping me out." With one last narrowed gaze at me, the two women hurried away.

"I don't know that I'll ever be able to repair the damage to my reputation," I said, half-joking because I didn't really care what these people thought of me.

Toni patted my arm. "I'll still be your friend. Weirdo."

I snorted a laugh. "I think Moe is behind this scarecrow. He's probably close by so he doesn't miss seeing the effects of his prank."

"Wasn't he supposed to be cheering people up, not freaking them out?" Toni said.

"He has a strange sense of humor." I walked around the scarecrow and turned the corner to find six stalls and a couple of sinks. I'd guessed right.

Moe was perched on the counter, his arms open in welcome. "Maybe it's your sense of humor that leaves something to be desired, pumpkin."

"Sure, Moe. Believe that." I didn't touch the glove in case it had evidence on it, like the murderer's fingerprint, if it was possible for fabric to hold a fingerprint. If the glove had been in the lake, then evidence might have washed away. Since I didn't know anything about forensics, I merely pointed at the glove. "Where did you find that glove, Moe?"

"He's here?" asked Toni. "What's he saying?"

"Yes, he's here. And nothing important yet."

Moe scratched his head. "Now, let me see. I got the clothes from a lost and found at that laundromat, the hat from a mariachi band, the blue glove in the middle of the road, and the one you like I found somewhere special." He winked.

"At the beach?"

"Nope. Not even close. Guess again."

"This is really important, Moe. Can you just tell me?"

He sighed. "Fine. I found that glove in a car, here in the parking lot. There was only one, so I snatched it."

I gasped. "Toni, he found the glove in a car here in the parking lot!" I turned to Moe. "Which car? Can you show us?"

"Sure can. Follow me." He disappeared.

"Wait!" I cried.

"What car?" Toni asked.

"I don't know. He said follow me, then he vanished. Come on!" I yanked the door open. "I hope he's out front."

I forced myself not to run through the lobby and draw attention. I burst through the main doors, my gaze sweeping the parking lot for Moe's blue hair and tiny red hat.

"Do you see him?" Toni asked, tugging on my sleeve.

"Not yet. Let's look around."

We crossed the driveway and scooted between two minivans to reach the middle of the lot. At the far end, there was Moe, waving his arms.

"I see him! Come on." We hurried to meet the ghost.

"Thank goodness the car is still here," I said. "Which one was it, Moe?"

"The Civic," he said, standing between two cars and indicating neither, as if I should know which was which.

"Which one is the Civic?" I asked, searching for a logo.

"It's the Civic?" Toni asked. "It's this one," she said, pointing at the silver one with a hatchback. Automobiles interested Toni, whereas I identified cars by their colors.

"Where was the glove, and how did you notice it?" I asked Moe.

"I noticed the car with a fond remembrance of my first wife. She drove the same model. She had a marvelous sense of humor and would have loved my scarecrow."

"Lovely sentiment," I said, not wanting to hear more. "So, you found the glove in this car? Was there only one glove?"

"Yes, indeed. Someone tossed it on the floor in the back. I figured that unless the driver was one-handed, they wouldn't miss it."

"His wife owned a car like this," I said to Toni. "The glove was on the back floor."

Toni took a photo of the car, and then one of the license plate. "Now, we have to find out whose car it is. Ask Moe when he found the glove."

Moe started to laugh. Soon he was doubled over.

"What's so funny?" I asked, getting a little worried by his reaction.

"Tell Toni I can hear her. What does she think I am, deaf?" He laughed again.

"It's not that funny," I said. "So, when did you find it?"

"Just a couple hours ago."

I relayed that to Toni. "Let's go back inside and see if the hotel management can tell us who owns that car."

Toni wandered around it, peering into the windows.

About to join her, Moe stopped me. "I'm not even going to ask why you care about that glove," he said. "Unless this car belongs to your new lover."

I rolled my eyes. "Good guess, but not even close."

"Pardon?" Toni asked. "Oh, never mind. You're talking to the clown. When we checked in, did you give them your license plate number?"

Thinking back, I didn't remember Courtney asking for it. "I don't think so."

"Me neither. So, they may not to be able to confirm who this car belongs to." Toni took my arm. "Well, let's go ask, anyway."

"Okay," I said. "Maybe we'll get lucky."

"Cheerio, pumpkin. I'll be with my scarecrow watching the giggles," Moe said and disappeared.

"I might need to borrow that glove!" I called into thin air, not knowing if he could hear me through the ether. A plan was coming together in my head, but the pieces weren't quite connected yet.

"Okay," Toni said. "You don't have to yell."

I was about to respond when my phone rang. "Give me a second. It might be Nell."

Toni nodded. "I'll meet you at the reception desk."

When I pulled out my phone, I saw it wasn't Nell. It was Alec, and as much as I wanted to talk to him, I couldn't take the time, so I let it go to voicemail. I needed to stay focused and figure how to trap a killer without revealing the reason I knew the glove was connected to a murder was because of a ghost and a dream vision.

I can do this. I've done it before.

A few minutes later, I found Toni showing the desk clerk the photo of the Civic. "Can you tell me who owns this car?"

"No, sorry," the clerk said. "We don't keep those records."

"It was a long shot," Toni said to me after thanking the woman. "So, I guess we're staking out the parking lot until the owner shows up."

"Yes, I guess so," I responded absently, distracted by a thought. "Hold on a sec. I need to text Nell."

When I'd finished, I looked at Toni. "Sorry, what were you saying?"

"We better hurry and figure out what we're going to do. The owner of the Civic could show up any minute."

"I think I've already figured it out. At least I have an idea. We'll have to watch for Nell, because she's part of our plan."

"She is?"

"Yep.

"Well, aren't you the smarty pants?" Toni said. "Or at least one of the smarty pants because I'm pretty sure I know whose car that is."

Chapter Twenty

"WHY DIDN'T YOU SAY so?" I asked when Toni told me she'd seen a bridal magazine on the passenger seat of the Civic.

"You were busy with the ghost and the glove, remember? I figured there could be someone else besides Courtney planning a wedding at this resort, so it made sense to ask at the front desk about the car first."

"Way to go! Okay. It's reasonable to say the car probably belongs to Courtney. Since she's looking like our strongest suspect, I think we should proceed accordingly."

"Accordingly, huh? Meaning you have a brilliant plan that ends with her confessing to Alicia's murder."

I hope so. "Yes, exactly." I said. *Confidence is empowering.* "Let's start with the scarecrow. We'll report the prank to Courtney, get her to come and see the scarecrow, and watch how she reacts to the glove."

Toni nodded. "Okay, that's a good start. If she used it to murder Alicia, the glove should startle her."

"Yes, it should. I'd like to wait for Nell, but someone else might report it to Courtney first, and then we'll lose the element of surprise."

"We'd better hurry," Toni said.

Heart to Heart's office door was open. I was relieved to see Courtney sitting at a desk, working on her computer. I rapped my knuckles on the door frame to get her attention. She looked up and smiled. "Hi, Quinn. What can I do for you?"

"I'm sorry to report another prank. It's upsetting people. Can you come and have a look?"

Courtney let out her breath and pushed her chair back. "What the—? Who's doing these things? It's got to be Becca." Courtney made an irritated sound. "What is it this time?"

"It's a scarecrow," I said, hoping that if she knew what to expect, she wouldn't be startled by the scarecrow itself, just the glove.

"Follow us," Toni said. "It's in the ladies' room."

We marched down the hall and across the lobby to the washrooms. I wanted to get in there first to see Courtney's reaction. Toni must have been thinking the same. She'd gotten ahead of us. I was behind her as she pushed the door open. Inside, I turned to face Courtney. "Here, it is."

She chuckled when she saw it. "Well, at least it's a happy scarecrow."

"It startled a couple of women," Toni said. "I'd say it's a bit of a mood dampener."

"Mood dampener?" came Moe's grumble from behind me. "What does she know? She's no clown."

I ignored Moe, keeping my eyes on Courtney, and said, "We should dismantle it before it upsets anyone else."

Moe jumped in front of the scarecrow.

Courtney's gaze narrowed. "Hey, wait a minute. I have gloves like that."

She'd admitted ownership of the glove! The look on her face was confused, but not the shock or horror I'd expect from someone who'd used the glove to murder Alicia.

I gasped as if I'd not noticed the glove before. *Push her harder.* "Good grief! Toni, didn't the police say they believed a glove with an orange stripe was connected to Alicia's death?"

Toni leaned forward to inspect the glove. "Yes, that's exactly what they said."

"What are you talking about?" Courtney asked.

Could I get her to reveal something incriminating? "Can we trust you to keep a secret?"

She blinked several times. "Okay. What secret?"

"Toni and I are investigating Alicia's death. There was cause to believe foul play was involved." Best not to mention the *cause* was my dream.

"Foul play?" Courtney looked truly stunned. "Are you suggesting someone murdered Alicia?"

Huh? I got a panicky feeling in my gut, a feeling that something was off because it seemed her reaction was genuine.

A phone rang. She reached into her sweater pocket. "It's Nell. Just a minute."

As I listened to Courtney tell Nell that she was in the ladies' room, Moe nattered about the merits of his pranks.

"Okay, I'll be there right away," said Courtney, then she disconnected. "Nell wants to see us in the office. The scarecrow will have to wait."

Why hadn't Nell answered my text?

Moe skittered alongside us as we walked to the office. "Maybe Nell wants to talk to you about your unwillingness to put your heart out there, Quinn?"

Oh brother. Maybe Moe could be useful, but I wasn't sure how. I gave him a wide-eyed, piercing look, hoping he'd realize something serious was happening.

Thankfully, he said, "Ah, there's something up."

When we got to the Heart to Heart office, Nell was pacing. She swallowed and asked Courtney to close the door behind us. "Courtney, I've just been to the police station."

She let out her breath and tugged on her long silver necklace. "Quinn told me. The police think Alicia's death wasn't an accident?"

Nell looked at me, then back at Courtney. "Yes, uh...also, someone from our office has stolen our clients' credit card numbers as well as their personal information. Do you have any idea how this could have happened?"

Her eyes flew wide. Mouth hung open. "What? No—no. I don't know anything about that." She shook her head emphatically. "Nothing. How could I?"

"There's no one else besides you who's had access to that information."

"I swear I don't know anything about it. I don't. Nell, please... You have to believe that."

"I want to believe it, Courtney. It's now a police matter. An officer will be here soon to talk to you."

She slumped back against the desk. "Oh, gosh. Oh, no. It wasn't me. It wasn't."

The uncomfortable feeling inside me was growing. Something wasn't right. "Nell, can I talk to you for a moment in private?"

Nell looked relieved. "Yes, certainly."

"Courtney, would you mind stepping outside the office?" I asked. "Perhaps you could deal with that scarecrow."

"Okay," she said, weakly.

As soon as she was outside, I glanced at Moe and said for his benefit, "We need to follow Courtney discretely and see what she does. If she's guilty of Alicia's murder, she'll make a move to protect herself."

"Guilty of Alicia's murder?" Moe asked. "I'm on her!" He disappeared through the door. I breathed a sigh of relief that he was on board.

"You think Courtney killed Alicia?" Nell said. "It's so hard to imagine her killing anyone." Nell paled and shook her head. "We can't all follow her—not discreetly."

"I'll go," I said, letting a few more seconds pass before opening the door.

The hallway was empty. I hurried to the end, stopping short to peer around the corner into the lobby. If Courtney went to the ladies' room, she'd have crossed the lobby first. By the front window, I saw Moe waving his arms and motioning me forward.

"She's outside," he said. "You stay here. I'll see what she's doing."

I could see her standing by the fire pit, raising her phone to her ear. She turned her back to the lobby and hunched over her phone. I saw Moe pop in beside her. Since she'd been warned, she could be innocently calling someone for advice. Or not.

It was killing me to wait, but I didn't have a choice. Minutes passed and finally she hung up. Moe cocked his head, watching her. *Come on, Moe! Tell me what she said.*

Another minute. I couldn't see what she was doing, but she hadn't moved. Was she making another phone call?

Moe popped in beside me. Finally. I had to remember I was in the lobby with a dozen other people.

"Well, that was interesting," he said and tapped his chin.

A woman moved closer to me. I stared into the clown's painted eyes. Raised my brow. *What, Moe?*

"Clowns are sometimes considered foolish, pumpkin, but in truth, we are great influencers. For instance—"

I cleared my throat. *No time for a lecture on fools!*

He frowned. Clicked his tongue. "For instance, I'm a good people-reader. I don't believe Courtney is the guilty party."

Why's that? I cocked my head.

"You're wondering why? Let me tell you. During her phone call—she was talking to someone named Dario—she didn't sound the way a murderer would sound. At least, I don't think so. She's baffled by Nell's

accusation and terrified she'll be accused of doing something she didn't do."

Okay. I was afraid of that. But just because Courtney
didn't do it—

"What's going on?" Toni said, having come up beside
me. "What's she doing out there?"

"Moe said she called Dario. She's not behaving like she's
guilty of anything."

"I'm not surprised she'd call her fiancée," Toni said.

With Toni beside me, I could talk to Moe without looking suspicious. "Moe, do you know what Dario told her to
do?"

"I sure do," he said, looking pleased with himself.

"Holy cow, Moe. You don't make things easy," I said.

"Fine, but easy isn't always best," he said. "The gentleman she calls Dario told her to meet him at hole three.
That would be the golf course, I presume."

"Why didn't you say so sooner?" I repeated Moe's words
for Toni.

"What's she doing now?" Toni asked.

"She's thinking it over, isn't she?" said Moe.

I caught sight of a man, dressed in black, moving quickly, approaching Courtney. He wore a baseball cap and
walked with his head down. When he reached her, they
started talking.

"Or she's waiting for someone," I said.

"Who's that?" asked Toni.

I was pretty sure I knew. "That's Bernardo."

"Oh?" said Toni. "So that's Bernardo. He looks like a
creep from here. Do you think she's in cahoots with him?"

Possibly. "Good question. Moe, go listen to what they're saying."

"I wonder if a snowman would have been jollier than a scarecrow," he said, looking up at the cumulus clouds.

"Never mind the scarecrow. Go, please. For Alicia."

"Okay, okay." He disappeared, but he was too late. Courtney and Bernardo were walking toward the golf course. We'd missed whatever they'd discussed.

"Let's follow them," I said. "If she's not in cahoots with Bernardo, she could be in danger."

We hurried out the door and followed behind, keeping a suitable distance between us. "I don't see Moe anywhere. I hope he's not gotten too preoccupied with his pranks to help us find his friend's killer."

"Not every ghost is reliable," Toni said, sounding like the voice of authority. I would have smiled if I wasn't so tense.

The path leading to the course took us through the forest. As we walked, I sent Nell a text telling her where we'd gone—at least I tried to write that. I wasn't proficient texting on the move. I hoped she'd be able to figure it out from the mistakes I didn't have time to change.

When we reached the end where things opened up onto a green, Toni and I hung back. Courtney and Bernardo had stopped close to the flag.

"This must be the third hole," Toni whispered.

"Let's get closer," I said, motioning toward the woods where we could sneak up closer and hide behind the brambly bushes.

We tiptoed carefully, so we wouldn't step on anything and draw their attention. Because it was slow going, Dario had joined them by the time we got close enough to hear.

"No!" Courtney said emphatically. "That's impossible. We can't go to Columbia right now. What about the wedding?"

Dario hesitated; looked at Bernardo. "We'll be back in time. We gotta go now, Court. My uncle needs me."

"Do you know how many details I still need to take care of? Not to mention leaving Nell in a lurch. She'll think I'm running away if I suddenly take off to Columbia."

"You better do as you're told," Bernardo said.

Courtney noticeably flinched. "Excuse me? Dario, are you going to let your cousin talk to me like that?"

I looked at Toni and mouthed cousin? Bernardo, who had threatened me, was Dario's cousin.

"Hey, she's right," Dario said to Bernardo. "Cool it. I'll handle this."

Bernardo clenched his fists. "You okay with disobeying my father? Gonna let your girlfriend tell you what to do?"

Dario seemed to pale. "Court, you gotta trust me. This is serious stuff. You want the house? The car? Then we gotta do what he says." Dario jerked his head toward Bernardo. "Come with me now, and I'll explain everything."

"You better explain everything," Courtney said, stepping forward. "In private," she said, glaring at Bernardo. Dario took her hand.

Courtney had nothing to do with stealing credit card numbers or clients' identities. I felt like my skin was electrified. *Don't let her leave with these men.* "Something is very wrong here," I whispered. "We have to stop her." I pushed a branch out of our way and pricked myself on a thorn. "Ouch. Thorns."

"Careful!" Toni said behind me.

The three people on the green turned at the sound of us stumbling out of the brambles. Another thorny branch scraped my forearm. "Courtney, can we talk to you for a sec?"

"Quinn?" Courtney looked perplexed. "Why were you in the bushes?"

"We were making sure you didn't do anything that might get you into trouble," Toni said.

"It's you," Bernardo said, glaring at me.

"Yes, it's me, Bernardo. We know about the stolen identities, and so do the police." I pointed to the resort at the bottom of the hill. "They'll be here any minute."

"What do you know about stolen identities?" Courtney asked Bernardo.

"I thought you did something about her," Dario said through his teeth.

Courtney dropped his hand. "What's that supposed to mean?"

"Don't you know who they are?" he asked.

Courtney looked at me, then at Toni. "Quinn and Toni?"

"They're the Murder Gals. I saw them in an article online. They think they're detectives."

Shoot. He'd seen that article in the Bookend Bay Bugle. Why didn't I think of that possibility? "So that's why Bernardo threatened me."

"Courtney's eyes widened.

"She thinks I killed Alicia," Dario said to Courtney.

I made a judgment call. Dario had come to Courtney's defense. Would he do it again? "No, I don't," I said. "We have proof to back up the police's theory that it was Courtney. She was stealing Heart to Heart's old clients' identities and Alicia found out."

Courtney gasped. Stepped back. "That's a lie! I didn't kill Alicia."

"All the evidence points to you," Toni said. "We know your gloves were used to kill Alicia, so you better get a lawyer."

"And you're right about Columbia," I said. "If you leave the country, you'll become a fugitive." I added for effect.

Bernardo grabbed my arm. "You're not showing any proof to anybody."

"He's got a gun," Toni said in a squeaky voice.

My skin turned to ice. This was the part I didn't love about being an apron-wearing crusader for justice. Things got a little sketchy when killers were accused of murder. I looked down the hill. *Nell, you'd better have read my message telling the police to hurry to the third hole.*

"Let her go!" Courtney cried. "What's going on, Dario? Did Bernardo...kill Alicia?"

"It wasn't me," Bernardo said. "We look after family. Do you want to be part of the family? Or would you rather rot in jail for something you didn't do? You're either with us or against us."

"What do you mean, look after family?" Courtney said. "Dario? What's he talking about?"

"He's right," Dario said. "We look after each other. Alicia was going to destroy everything. She threatened to hire an investigator. Go after me. My family."

"Go after your family for what?" Courtney said.

Dario shook his head. He wasn't giving details. *What will he do now?*

We needed a distraction. Some way to get the gun from Bernardo.

Moe appeared behind Dario, but I didn't feel a sense of relief at having the clown for a savior.

"Get ready. This is going to be amazing!" he said, moving beside Bernardo. "Keep your eyes here, pumpkin. You've got three seconds, then grab the gun. One. Two. Three!"

An explosive snap, crackle, pop cut through the air. Dario yelled, jumped, twisted. What was happening?

Keep your eyes here.

Bernardo. The gun!

Bernardo let go of my arm as he swung around and crouched. I kept my eyes on the gun. Moe karate chopped it out of Bernardo's hand. It hit the ground close to me. I snatched the gun, stepped back, and pointed it at Bernardo.

Courtney was screaming. Toni yanked Courtney away from Dario's side and pulled her to me.

"I'm burned!" Dario yelled, whipping his head around to look at his backside. Three firecrackers lay on the ground by his feet. Moe must have stuffed them in Dario's pocket.

"Oh no, the killer burned his bum!" Moe said, laughing. "The police are here, Murder Gal," he said to me and bowed dramatically. "No need to thank me. I'll leave you to finish up. I have a scarecrow to protect!"

Chapter Twenty-One

WHEN I WALKED IN the front door at Break Thyme, I knew right away that something was wrong. Or at least, something was missing. There was no rich coffee aroma wafting through the café to greet our customers when we opened.

Behind the counter, Ivy looked up, saw me, and threw up her hands. "I'm glad you're here. Maybe it'll listen to you."

What was she talking about? "Maybe what will listen to me?" I sat my purse down on a stool and came around the counter.

She stood in front of the coffeemaker, looked at me, then looked back at the machine. "Tell me what I'm doing wrong. Okay, coffeemaker, brew a full pot of coffee."

I stared at her. "What's supposed to happen?"

She looked at me like I was daft. "It's supposed to make the coffee. Or am I supposed to say hey, coffeemaker? Or does it like to be called something else?"

"Ivy, why do you think you have to talk to the coffeemaker?"

"Because it's voice-activated."

Now I gave her a look. "There's no such thing. What gave you that idea?"

"Your note. Didn't you leave this?" She picked up a tented card that said—the coffeemaker is now voice-activated.

I laughed. "No, I did not leave that note. The coffeemaker works the same way it's always worked." I pushed the brew button.

"Oh, man! I've been talking to that thing for the last twenty minutes. Somebody thinks they're real funny."

"Yep, a real clown," I said, looking around for Moe, but he wasn't visible. I hadn't seen him since that day on the Great Bear golf course when he'd stuffed firecrackers in Dario's pants and saved the day. I'd had to admit, his prank had worked.

When the police arrived, Bernardo gave Dario up in two seconds' flat. They took Dario in for questioning, then charged him with the murder of Alicia Smallwood.

The back door of the café opened and closed. A minute later, Poppy, tying her apron, came through the kitchen door. "Good morning, everyone. I smell scones, but where's the coffee?"

"It's not making itself, but it's coming," Ivy said, stepping away from the burbling machine.

Poppy sent Ivy a quizzical look, then she said to me, "Did you get Toni to the airport, okay?"

"Yes. I just dropped her off." After we solved Alicia's murder, I left the event and came back to work, but Toni stayed to see how things would pan out with Clark.

"I still can't believe she agreed to be on that show," Poppy said. "It all happened so fast. You don't think she'll come back married to Clark, do you?"

Heart to Heart had won the competition for the prime television special with the most love matches—one of which was Toni and Clark. At their victory party, Nell had celebrated with such enthusiasm, she'd lost her voice for a day. As soon as she recovered, she reported Melody's unethical behavior to the Event Planner's Association.

"No. She and Clark really fell for each other, but she has no desire to get married and told Clark that. They decided to do the show anyway and have an adventure. I think it will be a fun experience."

"I hope so," said Poppy. "I've watched a few of those falling-in-love reality shows, and there always seems to be back-stabbing and crying."

"I can't imagine Toni getting involved in any kind of drama."

"Me neither. Are you going to talk to her while she's away and see how things are going?"

"Nope. She can't talk about it until after the show airs, so we'll know nothing until then."

"Holy cow, Quinn. How are you going to manage that?"

Right. The unequaled Curious Me. It would kill me not to know what happened to Toni in Mexico, but I was going to have to buck up. "I'm going to keep my mouth shut and hate every second of it."

Poppy clicked her tongue. The bells over the door jingled. A couple of Bookend Bay's shop owners came in—Ollie and Ruby. It was time to get to work. I just hoped the day would pass quickly, because I was finally seeing Alec that night for our dinner date.

My mother taught me to love anticipation. She planned holidays well in advance, so as kids we had months before our vacations to anticipate and dream about them.

Since Alec and I both led busy lives, I'd been happily anticipating spending time with him.

I drove to his cabin on a lakefront lot he'd purchased for the new house he was building, having given up his marital home to his ex in their divorce settlement.

I knocked on the door and stood back when I saw him coming.

"There she is," he said, giving me a long hug. "I've been looking forward to this."

Mmm. I was so comfortable in his embrace that I could have moored there for the rest of the season, but that was rather unreasonable, so I stepped back and gave him the bottle of wine I'd brought.

"Thanks," he said, reading the label. "Perfect for dinner."

In the kitchen, he poured me a glass of wine. On the counter sat a bouquet of sunflowers. "I picked these up for you 'cause you make me feel sunny inside." He winked.

Sunflowers! Two thoughts hit me. First, he had a sexy wink and second, the last time I saw a vase of sunflowers, they didn't exist, at least not permanently.

"You bought me sunflowers." Anxiety flickered to life inside me. These flowers had to be real because he'd just mentioned them.

"Don't you like sunflowers?" he asked.

Could these be the same ones? They looked the same. I realized I had a weird look on my face. "Yes, I do! They're beautiful and what you just said was sweet. Thank you." The flowers were lovely, but I still couldn't bring myself to touch them. I hadn't been able to find any rhyme or reason to my apparitions. Even when I considered what Adelaide said, I still didn't know what need oils and sunflowers fulfilled. Ever since Dario was caught, the apparitions and my recurring dream stopped. Permanently, I hoped.

"You're welcome." He turned on the oven and flicked his head to the back door. "Let's sit outside while this heats up. I want to hear all about your murder case. Have I mentioned your life is a lot more interesting than mine? The only thing I accomplished over the last couple of weeks was fixing the park's water pump."

I smiled. "I consider water to be high on my priority list, so thank you for that."

Outside, we sat in the dappled shade of an old maple, and I told him all about finding Alicia's killer. Dario had admitted he'd followed Alicia that morning to her rowboat. The weather took a turn for the worst, and she'd changed her mind about going out, but by then it was too late. It was Dario who'd changed my date from Mac to Bernardo since he knew how to get into Heart to Heart's system, but he said he'd had nothing to do with the sprinklers going off at Lakeview Inn. I was leaving that mystery to their insurance company.

Becca Brewster called Nell to congratulate her and ask that they bury the hatchet and stop sabotaging each other. Becca had fired an employee when they admitted to spiking the punch at Great Bear.

Poor Courtney, who'd been innocent, had been hysterical the day Dario and Bernardo were arrested, but Nell said Courtney was recovering from the shock of it all and was taking a holiday with her sister.

In the time it took to tell Alec the story, he'd thrown something in the oven and had excused himself to run back inside and retrieve it.

"Stolen identities, huh," he said, placing a platter of cheesy toasts on the table between us. "What was Dario doing with them?"

"Good question, and since I have an overactive sense of curiosity, I got Deputy Cody to ask about that." Since Cody became Poppy's boyfriend, he'd been a decent source of information.

"And?" Alec said, offering me a napkin. "Better let these cool for a minute."

Okay, he was impressing me. The toasts looked to be prosciutto, pear, and brie, but there was also an aroma I couldn't place.

"Well, Dario was stealing identities from the people he did tech work for. In Heart to Heart's case, he'd also taken active credit card numbers that were collected when a debit machine malfunctioned. He was giving the identities to his uncle, who's a doctor in Columbia where they have a public health care program. Then the uncle made bogus claims for medical treatments he claimed he was performing on American expats. He'd bilked the systems for hundreds of thousands."

"I read something about this a few years ago." Alec shook his head. "It's a real problem in Columbia, where the justice system is also corrupt. This kind of thing can also be about funding political campaigns and illegally armed groups."

"It must be so frustrating for the people trying to do good work. As a physician, Dario's uncle is supposed to do no harm, yet his theft leaves his patients and other citizens suffering when there's no money for medicines or equipment."

Alec nodded. "Yep, guys like that have no conscience. You deserve a medal, Quinn. You caught the guy." He leaned in and took my hand.

I loved how he made me feel—significant, valued, savvy. "I can't take all the credit. There were Toni, Nell and the police in two countries"—not to mention Brielle and my new ghost-clown friend Moe—"but thank you."

"Since I don't have any medals handy, I can only offer you my roasted bruschetta with walnut oil, but I don't want to let your hand go just yet."

"Walnut oil? That's what I was smelling." *Holy cow. Sunflowers. Walnut oil.*

"Yeah. I love the stuff. I nearly cried when I dropped the bottle. Lost the whole thing."

That's what my visions had been about—Alec. He was what I needed in my life?

You're second-guessing something important. You need to trust yourself.

Trust that I was wiser than the young, inexperienced woman I'd been when I'd married a man who wasn't right for me. Trust that I would always look after my needs, never compromise my values, and always be my true self. How could I be in a relationship with Alec without being my authentic self? Would he want to give me a medal after I told him about the ghosts and Brielle?

One step at a time.

And since I didn't want to let his hand go either, we talked some more, letting the intimacy grow between us as our fingers intertwined, and we got acquainted with each other's touch.

For just a moment, my thoughts strayed to wild orchid massage oil and when it might make an appearance. I lingered in that possibility as we polished off the bruschetta.

Everything was delicious that night, the food, the company, the conversation. And when a pink ruffle on the other side of a cedar tree caught my attention, I looked over to see Brielle in a sun hat giving me a thumbs up, blowing a kiss, and disappearing into the sunset.

If you enjoyed A *Spirited Delusion*, join Quinn and Toni in their next adventure in A Spirited Accusation, book 6 in the Midlife is Murder series available on Amazon.

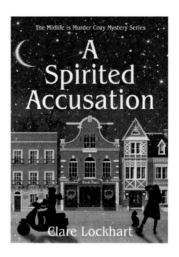

Quinn Delaney is struggling to keep mum about her paranormal midlife. Thankfully, she has her best friend Toni Miller to confide in.

Secrets between them are usually off limits.

Except, a non-disclosure agreement keeps Toni's lips sealed about outrageous events that happened during a reality show where she fell head over heels in love.

That secret is driving Quinn crazy.

She wants the best for her bestie, but when Quinn finds a Bookend Bay baker dead, she must rethink what's best when the baker's ghost points a finger at her murderer—the new love of Toni's life.

It can't be true!

But can Quinn take that chance and keep her friend safe while hunting for a killer?

Then the ghost of Toni's beloved husband enters the mix, and Quinn soon learns he's not the man she remembers.

Suddenly, she's the one keeping secrets from Toni.

As the two best friends follow a trail of clues to find the truth behind the baker's murder, Quinn worries if her friendship with Toni can survive the horrendous spirited accusation.

Grace and Frankie meet Murder She Wrote in this cozy, paranormal mystery with twists and turns that will keep you reading into the night! Get your copy on Amazon.

If you haven't already joined Clare Lockhart's newsletter for a FREE book, goodies, and exclusive news, please join here!Or on Clare's website: https://clarelockhart.com

Also by Clare Lockhart

Midlife is Murder
Paranormal Cozy Mystery Series
A *Spirited Swindler* (Book 1)
A *Spirited Debacle (Novella)* (Book 1.5)
A *Spirited Double* (Book 2)
A *Spirited Vengeance* (Book 3)
A *Spirited Betrayal* (Book 4)
A *Spirited Delusion* (Book 5)
A Spirited Accusation (Book 6)

Midlife is Magic
Paranormal Cozy Mystery Series
Visions and Villainy (Novella) (Book 1)
Curses and Consequences (Book 2)
Potions and Plunder (Book 3)
Scandals and Snafus (Short Story in A *Witch of a Scandal* anthology)
Sorcery and Suspects (Book 4)

Acknowledgments

Thank you to Irene Jorgensen for your friendship, your edits, and for the brain-storming sessions that always help make my stories more cohesive.

To my critique group: Carole Ann Vance, Linda Farmer, Sheila Tucker for your ongoing insightful feedback and for sticking with me and my endeavors for many years.

To my fabulous beta readers for catching pesky errors, inconsistencies, and more: Alan Pinck, Barb Stoner, Bobbi Radford, Cherie Moseley, Danette Fowlie, Jean Sparks and SW Knight. I so appreciate your time and support and for helping me publish a polished story.

And to John Burrows for being my champion, for helping me plot (fictional) murder, and for your attention to detail. I will be forever grateful for your rabbit-hole searches, for helping me climb marketing mountains, for proof-reading everything I write, and for your never-ending encouragement.

About the Author

Clare Lockhart grew up on Nancy Drew and paranormal stories from her dad who loved all things supernatural. She writes light-hearted, small-town, paranormal cozy mysteries featuring middle-aged sleuths who are going through a few changes. If you like reading about best friends who find themselves in the odd pickle, twisty murder plots that keep you guessing, and cheeky, paranormal visitors, then you'll love these fast-paced mysteries!

She would love to hear from you, so please send an email to clare@clarelockhart.com and visit https://clarelockhart.com/ to learn more about Clare and her books.

If you'd like to receive free content, hear the latest news, and stay in touch, please join: Clare Lockhart's Newsletterby clicking the link if you're reading an eBook. You can also join from Clare Lockhart's website at http://clarelockhart.com.

14155650R00131